"Look, this is how I see it," Pacey said. "Personally, I'm sick of hearing how teenagers don't care about anything and don't take any initiative. We can prove that wrong if we do our own fundraiser to save Dunn's Lighthouse."

"What did you have in mind, Pacey?" Emily called out.

Pacey peered down into the audience. "Jen?"

"What we were thinking of is a Teen Celeb-For-A-Day Auction," Jen said. "Some of us would volunteer to dress up as famous people. And then we'll hold an auction. Any teen can bid on the celebs, and the highest bidder gets to order that celebrity around for the day."

Everyone started talking at once, laughing about what celebrity they'd like to be with and/or order around for a day.

Dawson stood and said, "I just wanted to say that I think Pacey and Jen's idea is great. I volunteer to video the whole thing. We can make copies, sell the video, and raise even more money."

# Dawson's Creek™

## Too Hot to Handle

Based on the television series "Dawson's Creek"™
created by **Kevin Williamson**

Written by C. J. Anders

**POCKET BOOKS**
New York London Toronto Sydney Tokyo Singapore

This book is a work of fiction. Names, characters, places and incidents are products of the author's imagination or are used fictitiously. Any resemblance to actual events or locales or persons living or dead is entirely coincidental.

An *Original* Publication of POCKET BOOKS

 POCKET BOOKS, a division of Simon & Schuster Inc.
1230 Avenue of the Americas, New York, NY 10020

ISBN: 0-671-03528-2

First Pocket Books printing August 1999

10  9  8  7  6  5  4  3  2  1

POCKET and colophon are registered trademarks of Simon & Schuster Inc.

DAWSON'S CREEK is a registered trademark of Columbia TriStar Television, Inc.

Printed in the U.S.A.

For our buds in Nashville: we miss you!

# Too Hot to Handle

# Chapter 1

"**B**elieve me when I say that being dragged away from the onerous task of hand-washing my father's truck is motivation enough to be out here traipsing through swamp grass with you two," Pacey Witter told his friends, Dawson Leery and Jen Lindley. "But just out of curiosity, where are we going?"

"Dunn's Lighthouse, Pacey," Jen replied, swatting away some dive-bombing mosquitos. "I'm doing the interview, and the blond guy next to you—allegedly your best friend—the one lugging the video equipment, is doing the filming. Try to keep up."

"Dunn's Lighthouse," Pacey echoed, stepping over an overturned log. "All righty, then, boys and girls. Let's review. There I was, soapy washrag in hand, about to apply said rag and soap to said beyond-filthy Ford truck, when the two of you accosted me, kidnapped me, forced me into the car—"

"We asked if you wanted to come along," Dawson corrected. "That does not constitute use of force."

"*Forced* me into the car," Pacey repeated, "which is exactly what I'll tell Sheriff Witter, also known as Dear Ol' Dad, when he demands to know why his Ford and joy remains unwashed. And brought me out here to this godforsaken swampland to look for Bigfoot."

"*Bickfee*, not Bigfoot," Jen said. "Her name is Quinn Bickfee. Bigfoot is just what the people who side with the developers call her. As in picket signs that say 'Butt Out, Bigfoot.' "

Pacey wiped some perspiration from his forehead. It wasn't yet eight in the morning, and already the day was stifling. "How far do we have to walk to get to the lighthouse?"

"Half mile or so," Dawson said.

Pacey rolled his eyes. "I shoulda stuck with the truck."

Jen nudged him playfully with her elbow. "Come on, Witter. Aren't you even curious? Quinn refuses to let anyone over the age of nineteen interview her because she says all adults are corrupt. And supposedly she turns away most teen reporters, too—"

"So—" Pacey interrupted, "why—"

"Unless she likes their aura," Jen finished.

"Aura you into that crap?" Pacey joked.

Jen winced.

"Not punny," Dawson said, trying not to laugh.

"You're right," Jen agreed. "And what I'm into is getting the interview. Period."

2

"Call me crazy, but wouldn't Lighthouse Girl want all the press she can get?"

"The more difficult she makes it to interview her, the more everyone wants to," Jen explained.

"Which is brilliant, in a perverse, calculated kind of way," Dawson said, as he gingerly stepped over a muddy hole.

Jen nodded. "I'm hoping that we're showing up so early that no other reporters are there. And that she'll give us the interview. And that I'll find a way to get it on the air."

Dawson smiled at her. "You've really turned into a producer, Jen."

"Reporter/producer," Jen corrected. "And when I win my first Emmy—Oscar, whatever—I'll be sure to mention Dawson Leery, who gave me my break when he forced me to produce one of his first films."

"Ah, yes." Pacey nodded. "Leery's late adolescent Capeside period. Pivotal in truly understanding the underlying theme of his later genius."

"I should be taking notes," Dawson said.

"It was where Leery, like Capra and Spielberg before him," Pacey expounded in a fake academic voice, "developed his almost childlike belief that love lost can result in love found once more. Hanky, please, I'm weeping."

Jen glanced at Dawson as they worked their way through the tall grass. His face had tightened up, and a muscle was working in his jaw. Clearly, Pacey's teasing had hit a little too close to home. Dawson's love lost was Joey Potter, the girl he had known forever. The girl who was not speaking to him. The girl who maybe would never speak to him again.

"Hey, let's lighten up this little parade, huh?" Jen suggested. "Want to go swimming later?"

"Andie loves to swim," Pacey muttered, his voice low.

Andie. As in Andie McPhee. As in the love of Pacey's life, now in Providence with her dictatorial father and emotionally unbalanced mother. And Andie, with the psychological problems that had resulted from—

Well. Anyway, no one knew when or if Andie would ever come back to Capeside.

It was killing Pacey.

*Boy gets girl, boy loses girl,* Jen thought. *Third act has yet to be written.*

"You know, Pacey, you and Dawson should be coaxing Ingmar Bergman to come out of retirement and make a movie about you both," Jen said. "One of you is hung up on a girl who's physically absent, the other one is hung up on a girl who's emotionally absent."

"As opposed to you, who is hung up on being hung up," Pacey added.

Jen laughed. "Our wallowing is so banal."

"I agree," Pacey said. "So let's do something more dramatic. Throw ourselves on our swords, maybe. Did we bring swords?"

"Sword-free," Dawson told him, as the three of them slowed in order to wend their way across a plank that had been set over a small stream. "And I am not pining."

4

Jen's eyebrows went up. "What would you call it?"

"The third act crisis in a love story with a happy ending," Dawson said firmly. He stepped off the plank and sank into the muddy ground nearly to his ankles. "Yecch!"

Pacey clapped him on the back, as he stepped off the plank. "Let's hope your third act crisis doesn't last longer than, say, the director's cut of *Meet Joe Black*."

*Or,* Jen thought, *let's hope that you finally get over Joey and . . . and what? It isn't like I still want Dawson. It's just that wanting him is a hard habit to break.*

When she'd first moved to Capeside from New York, she and Dawson had been an item. But she'd been so busy trying to escape her dark past in New York, trying to figure out who she really was, that she hadn't been ready to be in any kind of a relationship, much less one with a guy as genuine and romantic as Dawson Leery.

And now . . .

Jen sighed. They were great friends. Somewhere out there was the right guy for her. Not her old boyfriend from New York, Billy. Not the guy she'd been seeing for a while in Capeside, Ty.

And not Dawson.

Except that she couldn't quite forget how it had felt when Dawson's pure love had erased all the bad stuff that had happened in New York, had made her feel clean and pure and hopeful again, had . . .

*Forget it, girl,* Jen told herself now. *He and Joey*

*may be a noncouple. But his heart still belongs to her.*

*It's all so excruciatingly daytime drama,* Jen thought wryly. *Joey the local good girl, Dawson the sensitive romantic, and Jen the bad girl from New York.*

"So, now that we've wallowed in our own personal melodramas, allow me to change the subject," Pacey said. "How do you plan to get Bigfoot to let you interview her?"

"Ask," Dawson said, shrugging.

Pacey pointed at him. "You're good." He fisted his hand and held it under his mouth like a microphone. "We're on our way through the swamp, risking typhus, malaria, Ebola, and the wrath of one Sheriff Witter, whose truck remains encrusted in crud, to get an interview with one Quinn Bickfee, aka the Lighthouse Girl, aka Bigfoot."

Jen played along, speaking into her own fist. "Quinn Bickfee, eighteen, reasonably photogenic ecological activist, has been perched in the uppermost portion of Dunn's Lighthouse, in the picturesque coastal town of Capeside, Massachusetts, for ten days now. She is protesting the scheduled destruction of the historic lighthouse by the Woodman Corporation, which plans to build an upscale beach resort and shopping mall at the site. Asked in an earlier interview what Ms. Bickfee would like to say to the developers, she replied, 'Woodman, spare that lighthouse!' "

"Ouch," Dawson said, wincing.

Pacey laughed. "The mighty Quinn allows no one into the lighthouse. She has no electricity, no sanitary facilities, and eats only raw food sent up to her on a pulley by an ardent band of admirers," he went on. "Ms. Bickfee has become the darling of photographers, who vie for the opportunity to photograph her in her perch atop the lighthouse. How fortunate for Bigfoot's cause that she resembles Liv Tyler, pre-haircut."

"So Liv stars in her life story?" Dawson asked.

"Too obvious," Jen mused. "Sarah Michelle Gellar?"

"I'm thinking Tori Spelling," Pacey mused.

"Tori Spelling *is* Quinn Bickfee!" Jen said dramatically.

"Cynicism oozes from every pore of your deeply jaded selves," Dawson said lightly. "I happen to admire her. Quinn, that is. I admire her for trying to save Dunn's Lighthouse. It's one of the oldest on the coast. Can you imagine the things it's seen? It would be a crime to rip it down."

Jen gave Dawson a skeptical look. "No offense, Dawson, but everything old is not valuable simply by virtue of its being old."

"I'll grant you that. But do you really want to see Dunn's Lighthouse bulldozed into smithereens just so some developer can make millions?"

"Depends," Jen mused. "Do I get a free suite at the new hotel?"

Pacey laughed and Dawson shot him a dirty look. "I can understand Jen making jokes about this. She didn't grow up here like we did. There's no reason she should feel any particular emotional attachments to Capeside. But your family has lived here forever, Pacey."

"A fact that does not make me hold Capeside near and dear to my heart, my man," Pacey replied. "As soon as I graduate from what is dubiously known as Capeside High School, I will beat all speed records in my race for the border."

"Are you telling me you feel no attachment whatsoever?" Dawson asked. He stopped walking. The lighthouse was now only a few hundred yards away.

Pacey gave him a level look. "What's Capeside?"

Dawson sighed. "Okay, I acknowledge that Capeside can be limiting at times. And I know that your relationship with your family hasn't been ideal—"

"Your powers of observation boggle the mind, Dawson," Pacey said.

"But we had some great times here when we were growing up. Remember that summer you and me and Joey caught all those fireflies and let them loose in my bedroom—"

"You and Joey."

"You were there, Pacey. I distinctly remember you jumping up and down on my bed, waving your arms at them—"

"And I distinctly remember my father showing up to drag me home by the ear, yelling about how stupid I was, right in front of you and Joey. Making me feel about two inches tall. Anyway, it was always Dawson and Joey. Pacey was the screwup sidekick afterthought. Even then."

"Much as you enjoy that particular little image of yourself, Pacey, you're no screwup anymore," Jen reminded him. "And it's not Dawson and Joey anymore, either. Things can change." Her eyes slid over to Dawson to see how he'd react to her remark.

He didn't.

"We're almost there" is all he said. Meaning almost to the lighthouse. Meaning he wasn't going to give Jen a clue as to what he was thinking about Joey.

"Hey, there she is, up there. See?" Pacey squinted into the distance. Quinn hung out the window, taking in the morning sunshine. "Amazing that she retains that bouncin' and behavin' hair under those conditions. What a woman."

He waved wildly, then bellowed through cupped hands, "Hey, Quinn! 'What light through yonder window breaks?' "

"Slick," Jen muttered.

"What, seeing her up there isn't a *Shakespeare in Love* kinda moment?" Pacey asked. "You know what really bugged me about that movie, other than the fact that I wasn't the one swapping spit with Gwyneth? The guy who owned the Globe Theatre kept saying that everything would end happily because it was a magical mystery. Only it didn't. Gwyneth and the Bard—"

"Do you have any idea how much you sound like Andie right now?" Dawson interrupted.

The smallest, saddest of smiles fit itself onto Pacey's lips.

"The McPhee stream-o'-consciousness rave," Pacey mused.

Dawson patted Pacey on the arm. "I kind of miss it, too."

"Let's hope Andie gets back really soon," Jen said. "Or else Pacey reverts to being . . . Pacey."

"Maybe Bigfoot can send Andie smoke signals

from the lighthouse," Pacey said. "Andie: Come Home."

They started walking again and cleared the high reeds that blocked their view of the lower part of the lighthouse.

"Listen, I suggest you let me do the talking," Jen said. "So far, she's only given interviews to women."

"Even in my lovelorn state I can see that you have the advantage there," Pacey noted. "As for my man Dawson over there, everything female has been rendered neuter until his true love decides to—"

He stopped.

Because Dawson's true love was sitting a few feet from the lighthouse, a sketch pad on her lap.

Joey.

Joey was drawing Quinn, who sat high above on a wooden ledge outside the lighthouse, her legs dangling, her long, dark hair blowing in the breeze.

Joey looked as startled to see them as they were to see her. She quickly closed her sketch pad so they couldn't see her work.

"Well, this calls for the trite. How about, small world and all that," Jen said to her.

Joey got to her feet and pushed her long brown hair out of her eyes nervously. "What are you guys doing here?"

"A question I was just about to ask," Quinn called down. She was standing now, on the ledge.

Jen pushed her sunglasses up into her tousled blond hair and peered up at Quinn. "Hi," she called. "I'm Jen Lindley. I was hoping I could talk to you."

"Who're the *males*?" Quinn asked, peering down at them.

"I'm Dawson Leery," Dawson called. "And this is my friend, Pacey Witter."

"You know them?" Quinn yelled down to Joey.

Joey nodded. Quinn just stood there.

"You're here to draw Quinn?" Dawson asked Joey.

Joey didn't answer him, quickly gathering up her stuff.

"It was a simple question, Joey," Dawson said. "If speaking to me is so painful, pretend someone else asked."

"I came out here at dawn a few mornings ago," Joey said, buckling closed her portfolio, not even glancing in Dawson's direction. "We talked. I asked if I could draw her. She said yes. The end."

"So where are you going? You can stay," Dawson said.

"Don't leave just because we're here," Jen added.

"Right," Quinn called down. "Just leave."

Joey looked up at Quinn. "I was planning to leave in a few minutes anyway. But I'll see you soon, if it's still okay."

"It's still okay," Quinn said. "That applies to you, only, I might add."

"I'd really like to understand why you're doing what you're doing," Jen cupped her hands and called to Quinn.

"Oh yeah, sure," Quinn said. "You're supposed to start out by telling me how much you admire me and agree with me and all that bull," Quinn said.

"Then I'm supposed to believe it. And that's how you get an interview."

Jen shrugged. "I admire that you're taking a stand about something you care about passionately. But whether or not I agree with you is irrelevant. And sucking up to you—or anyone else, for that matter—is not really my style."

Quinn laughed. "It's not my style, either. Joey?"

"Yeah?"

"What's up with them?"

"They're fine," Joey assured her. "They're friends."

"Friends, huh? Well, I trust you, Joey, so . . ." Quinn thought a second. "Okay. We'll try it. Briefly."

"Thanks," Jen shouted. She turned to Joey. "And thanks for vouching for us."

"Whatever." Joey slung her ratty backpack over one shoulder. "Listen, Quinn is really . . . I like her. What I'm saying is, this is not an opportunity to jump-start your career at her expense."

Jen stared hard at her. "You really think any of us would do that?"

"Joey?" Dawson took a step toward her. Her eyes met his. They were guarded.

*As in Joey doesn't live here anymore*, Dawson thought sadly. *At least not when it comes to Dawson Leery*.

"Just because you and I are . . . where we are right now," Dawson began, "doesn't mean that I'm not still fundamentally the same person you once cared about."

"One thing I've figured out, Dawson," Joey said, pushing her hair off her face. "Who we think anyone is, fundamentally, might be nothing more than who we need them to be. Have fun. Don't take advantage of her."

"Joey—"

But with a wave goodbye to Quinn, Joey was gone.

# Chapter 2

**Meeting Tonight: T.A.C.T.I.C.S.**
**Teens Against Corporations Trashing Idyllic Capeside's Seaside. Help Save Dunn's Lighthouse. Capeside High School Auditorium. 8 P.M.**
**• Let Your Voice Be Heard •**

*J*oey stood outside the high school nervously fingering the flyer she'd picked up at the restaurant where she was waitressing for the summer. The flyers, on hot-pink paper, had begun appearing all over Capeside two days earlier. She had no idea who was behind T.A.C.T.I.C.S.

*Probably one of the rah-rah types at school,* she figured. *Cheerleader. Maybe in student government. Hotshot football star b.f. Or else one of the counterculture huggie-veggie girls, some Paula Cole wannabe, who daily mourns the fact that she missed out on Woodstock. Numbers one and two.*

*Or else—*

Joey stopped her train of thought. Callously sticking people into little boxes was easier than facing her own nervousness about going into the meeting.

She bit her lower lip and watched a few kids run up the steps to the school. There were no signs of a huge crowd gathering. And Joey really did believe in saving the lighthouse. She'd spent some more time with Quinn, sketching her portrait, and now felt a certain loyalty to both the girl and the cause.

But Joey was so *not* a join-in-and-go-to-meetings kind of babe. Her one attempt at getting involved in student government with Andie had been so awful that . . .

She stuffed the flyer into the back pocket of her jeans and headed for the front door of the school and then slid into the back of the auditorium.

The turnout was not impressive at all. There were maybe two dozen kids wandering around up front, overwhelmed by the emptiness of the hall. A boombox on stage blared out the Grateful Dead's "Uncle John's Band."

Swell. Whoever had started T.A.C.T.I.C.S. was a deadhead.

"What are you doing here?" a voice demanded.

Joey looked next to her.

And down.

Dina Wolfe, who couldn't be more than twelve, was scowling up at her. Dina was Chris Wolfe's little sister. Chris considered himself the Studboy of Capeside High. Rich and handsome, the kind of guy who got off on the chase, he'd been with more girls than Joey could count.

Including Jen.

He'd also dropped more girls than Joey could count.

Including Jen.

But little sister Dina was as awkward as Chris was smooth. She was also geeky. With braces. And unattractive glasses. And she had the world's biggest crush on Dawson. Joey had once befriended Dina— she knew all too well what it felt like to be an angst-ridden preteen since she'd been one herself.

But these days, Dina considered Joey the competition.

For Dawson.

There was a certain irony to that.

"Hi, Dina, nice to see you, too," Joey said pleasantly. "How's your summer going?"

"That does not follow as a logical response to my question." Dina pushed her glasses up her nose.

"True," Joey agreed. She pointed to the flyer in Dina's hand. "Helping to save the lighthouse?"

Dina crossed her arms and narrowed her eyes. "I just want you to know, the seat next to him is already taken." She turned and flounced down the aisle.

*Him* means Dawson, Joey realized.

Her eyes followed Dina down the aisle, and she saw that Dawson was sitting on the back of a chair in the second row, talking to Jen. Joey was instantly convinced that their motivation for being at this meeting must have nothing to do with preserving the lighthouse.

Joey was torn—should she slink out so that she

wouldn't have to see Dawson or should she stay for a meeting about something that was important to her? At the front of the auditorium, Jen laughed loudly and put her hand on Dawson's arm as she said something to him that Joey couldn't hear.

Joey sighed.

*Same old, same old,* Joey thought. *Jen is still everything I am not. She is walking sex. And I am . . . just plain walking.*

She was outta there. She turned around to leave, but at that moment the door opened and Jack walked in.

Great. Her evening was getting better by the millisecond.

When she and Dawson broke up, she'd almost instantly gotten involved with Jack McPhee. Andie's brother. Sensitive, smart, loner Jack. Jack who was as much an outsider as Joey was.

Jack who wasn't Dawson.

Jack who had turned out to be gay.

Joey was over that little revelation. And now she and Jack were friends. Good friends. She was sure, really sure, that his being gay, and her not knowing he was gay, had nothing at all to do with her. Or how sexy she was. Or wasn't.

"Hey, how's it going?" Jack asked easily.

Joey arched one eyebrow. "You have a thing for lighthouses I didn't know about?"

"One of my many deep, dark secrets. That, and Jen asked me to come."

"Your roomie," Joey said lightly. She knew it shouldn't bother her that Jack was now living with

Jen and Jen's grandmother, right next door to Dawson, but it did. All these cozy little friendships.

Minus Joey.

As if Jack could read her mind, he said, "Would it be news to you that Jen cares about you?"

"Would it be news that what Jen Lindley does or does not care about is not exactly paramount in my sordid little life right now?"

Jack tugged playfully on a hank of Joey's hair. "Come on. I think we can go sit down there without risking our status as scandalous and brooding outsiders."

Joey laughed in spite of herself. "Only for you would I do this, Jack."

They headed down the aisle, taking seats a few rows behind the others. Joey took a moment to look around to see who this meeting had attracted. Sure enough, as she'd suspected, the counterculture huggie-veggie set was heavily represented as well as student leaders and assorted rah-rah types. And some of the certified brains, too, like Emily LaPaz, who was one of the top students in their class. Abby used to make fun of the size of Emily's butt.

And now Abby was dead.

Life was just so bizarre.

Joey leaned over to Jack. "So tell me, who is the mastermind behind this little—"

Before Joey could finish her question, she got the answer, as none other than Pacey strode out onto the stage.

*Pacey?*

"Hi, everyone," Pacey said into the microphone. "I guess you all know who I am. And now that you know I'm the one behind T.A.C.T.I.C.S., I guess you also know why I didn't put my name on the flyers."

There was some good-natured laughter.

"Yo, righteous Dead music, dude!" someone yelled.

"Frankly, the musical interlude was chosen by Jason over there," Pacey said, cocking his head toward a white guy with long dreadlocks and shorts so baggy they could house a family of four.

"As you all know," Pacey went on, "the Woodman Corporation plans to buy the land surrounding Dunn's Lighthouse, raze the lighthouse, and build a resort and an upscale shopping mall."

"Boo-o-o," Jason the Deadhead called out.

"There's already a legal petition to have it declared a protected area," Pacey went on, "but like most court maneuvers, it takes time. And that girl Quinn is up in the lighthouse. But Woodman's plan is to buy the land before a restraining order can come through to stop them, and then do what needs to be done to get Quinn out."

"They suck!" an alt type yelled.

"Deeply," Pacey agreed. "Woodman's closing the sale in exactly one week. There's only one way to stop them. Raise enough money to buy the land from the Dunn family before Woodman can buy it."

Joey leaned in to Jack. "If he's hitting us up for donations, I'm good for about a buck fifty."

A pretty brunette sitting off to the side with four friends waved her hand in the air. Joey vaguely recognized her—Kristy or Misty or something. She lived in one of the mansions on the hill overlooking Capeside, and she used to come into the Ice House sometimes in the summer with her friends. They all went away to private boarding school.

*And they spend about eighty percent of the rest of the time in New York City,* Joey recalled. *What are they doing here?*

"Yes?" Pacey nodded at her.

She jumped up and turned to the group. "In case you don't know me, I'm Bitsy Bannerman, and these are some of my friends. We've all lived in Capeside forever, but we go to boarding school in Switzerland, so I have to admit that we're not around much."

Joey and Jack traded looks and eye rolls.

"Anyway," Bitsy went on, "my parents, Barbi and Bill Bannerman, are very involved in saving Dunn's Lighthouse. They know the Dunns, who live in California now. You may have heard that my folks are giving a cocktail party on our yacht Saturday night, eightish, and there will be a silent auction of all kinds of things that have been donated, and all the proceeds will go to saving the lighthouse."

Bitsy waited for someone to say something, or applaud, or do something, but there was no response. Gamely, she pressed on.

"The night's called Summer Lights to Save the Lighthouse. It's open to the public. Admission is fifty dollars per person. There'll be dancing at sea under the moonlight to the Glen Hampton Orchestra, dessert, and champagne. Oh, it's black tie, by the way; for those of you who don't know, that means it's formal—tuxes and long gowns, please. And, as I said, all proceeds will go toward saving Dunn's Lighthouse."

"Why don't her parents just write a big, fat check and get the whole thing over with?" Jack asked Joey.

Joey shrugged. Girls like Bitsy fascinated her in some sick kind of way. It was like they were another species, they were so foreign.

"So," Bitsy went on, "my friends and I came to your little meeting to make sure you know about my parents' fund-raiser for the lighthouse. We think that what makes sense is for everyone here to work on our fund-raiser. I'm in charge of the teen volunteers, and I'd be happy to tell you what you can do to help make the silent auction and cocktail party under the stars a winner and save Dunn's Lighthouse."

She began to applaud, nodding at her friends to join her, and they did.

"Super," Bitsy chirped. "So, I move to adjourn this meeting and everyone who wants to work with me can—"

"Excuse me, Bitsy," Pacey interrupted. "Anyone who wants to work with you on the other fund-raiser can talk to you later. Right now I'd like to get back to talking about what it is that we—"

"Excuse *me*," Bitsy said, "but do you really think it's productive to plan some silly little tag sale or bake sale or car wash?"

"I don't think that's what Pacey has in mind," Dawson said. "And I'd also like to point out that a lot of people, and certainly most teenagers, can't afford the fifty-dollar admission to your parents' party. And they definitely can't afford to bid on anything at the silent auction."

"And I left my long gown at the dry cleaners," Emily LaPaz added sarcastically.

"If it's a money thing, my parents will allow teens who help plan the fund-raiser to attend for half-price," Bitsy explained. She turned to Emily. "And you can probably pick up a formal at Goodwill or something. I'm sure they carry larger sizes. Stick to basic black."

Jack leaned in to Joey. "You think she's channeling Abby's spirit?" he whispered.

"Okay, so it's settled, then!" Bitsy said perkily. "Everyone who wants to work with me can—"

"Excuse me, Bitsy," Pacey interrupted. "Anyone who wants to take you up on your really *keen* offer can meet with you anytime they want to meet with you, except now. To continue. This will be our own thing, done by teens for teens, adult input is strictly thanks, but no thanks. And any money *we* raise will be combined with the money of any other fund-raising efforts. So long as the money goes to a not-for-profit organization that will buy the land."

"Yeah," said Jason the Deadhead. "We don't want some rich person raising money for a good cause and then building a shopping center anyway!"

Bitsy jumped up again, and scowled at Jason. "But what's the point of having two different projects? My parents happen to be very experienced fund-raisers, okay? My mother was on the board of the New York City Ballet."

"No kidding?" Jen marveled. "I guess that means she worked for my aunt, who was chairwoman of the board."

Some kids laughed. Bitsy sat down huffily.

"Look, this is how I see it," Pacey said. "Personally, I'm sick of hearing how teenagers don't care about anything and don't take any initiative. We can prove that wrong if we do our own fund-raiser. Our ideas, our initiative, our work. And all the money to be donated to a nature conservancy group that buys up land for the purpose of preserving it."

"What did you have in mind, Pacey?" Emily called out.

Pacey peered down into the audience. "Jen?"

Jen hurried up onto the stage. "Hi," she said self-consciously. "I'm Jen Lindley. When I lived in New York, we once raised money for the Special Olympics by getting celebrities to donate stuff of theirs that we could auction off. But we got the most money when Courtney Love volunteered to let us auction *her* off. You know, for a day. The highest bidder got to ride around in her limo, go backstage with her at her concert, have dinner with her, like that."

"Did you arrange for Hole to come to Capeside?" Bitsy quipped nastily.

"I wish," Jen admitted. "What we were thinking of is a Teen Celeb-For-A-Day Auction. Some of us would volunteer to dress up as famous people. And then we'll hold an auction. Any teen can bid on the celebs, and the highest bidder gets to order that celebrity around for the day."

Bitsy jumped up. "Pacey?"

With a long-suffering sigh, "Yes, Bitsy?"

"Okay, that's a stupid idea. You're never going to raise enough money. No offense."

"Coming from you, Bitsy, none taken," Pacey said.

Jen leaned back into the microphone. "I don't think it's stupid. Imagine making Felicity clean your entire house."

"Or getting to pie the Olsen twins," Emily added.

Everyone started talking at once, laughing about what celebrity they'd like to be with and/or order around for a day.

Dawson stood up to speak, but everyone was still talking. Dina stood on her chair, whistled shrilly through her front teeth, and yelled, "SHUT UP!"

Startled, they actually did.

Dina sat, triumphant.

"Thanks." Dawson gave her a bemused look. "I just wanted to say that I think Pacey and Jen's idea is great. I volunteer to video the whole thing. We can make copies, sell the video, and raise even more money."

Most people began to murmur their enthusiasm.

Bitsy folded her arms and whirled on Dawson. "Excuse me, what's your name?"

"Dawson. Dawson Leery."

"Dawson Leery. Well, Dawson Leery, let me enlighten you. See, dressing up like Steven Spielberg doesn't mean you *are* Steven Spielberg, okay? No one is going to pay money for a cheesy little home video of pretend celebrities, no offense."

"Thanks for the enlightenment," Dawson said, nodding seriously. "By the way, did your parents hire someone to video Summer Lights to Save the Lighthouse on Saturday night?"

"Of course," Bitsy said crossly. "They hired *professionals:* Screenplay Videos."

Pacey hit himself in the forehead. "Screenplay Videos? Why didn't you say so? They're the best! No joke. I hear they did a sweet sixteen at the Plaza in New York that was so spectacular everyone is still talking about the impression they made."

Bitsy looked smug. "So you see, even Pacey has heard of them. Maybe I can persuade my mother to talk to them about doing your little thing, too, though I doubt you can afford them."

"Uh, Bitsy?" Jen began. "I hate to break this to you. But Dawson and Pacey *are* Screenplay Videos. And I'm their associate."

Everyone laughed. Bitsy smiled at Jen, utterly disbelieving her. "Of course Screenplay is Dawson and Pacey. And I'm sure you work . . . under them. All they had to do was ask you, right?"

"Right," Jen replied.

"Doesn't surprise me," Bitsy said, shrugging. "You've got the rep. In fact, I heard that you'll do anything that *any* guy asks you to do."

Jen's face turned stormy as Bitsy and her friends laughed.

Jack stood up. "What's your problem?" he asked Bitsy. "So your rich parents are giving a fund-raiser for their rich friends on your rich yacht. Fine. Have a great time. What I don't get is why you're trying to wreck this one when it's for the same cause?"

"We've heard all about you, too, Lisp-Boy," Bitsy said. "What's the matter, afraid you'll have to save your Judy Garland outfit until the next pride parade in New York City?"

Before Joey could even think about what she was doing, she had gotten up, gone down the aisle, and got right in Bitsy's face.

"Listen, Bitsy, before you decide to turn your viper tongue on me, yes, I am *that* Joey Potter, and I've already heard much better insults than your pea-sized brain could possibly conjure up, though it's sweet that you try so hard, and fail so miserably. And now, on behalf of every teenager in Capeside who is actually gauche enough to live here year 'round and, yes, even go to public school here, we would really appreciate it if you and your sycophantic band of mindless muppets just got your butts out of here. Now. Oh, no offense."

Derisive laughter rang through the auditorium as Bitsy turned the same color as her cherry-red sundress. "Listen you little—what?"

Bitsy whirled around as someone tapped her on the shoulder. It was Jen, who had come down from the stage.

"Lovely chatting with you, Bitsy," Jen said. *"Ciao."*

"How dare you touch—"

Jen took her arm. "You were just leaving, right?"

"Okay, okay!" Bitsy jerked herself from Jen's grip and whirled around to glare at her. "Anyone who wants to join a fund-raiser run by a loser, stay in your seats by all means. Anyone with brains, taste, or class can call me. I'll leave cards with my phone number on them on the table at the back of the room. Come on, we're leaving," she told her friends.

They dutifully followed Bitsy down the aisle. Bitsy

26

dropped a bunch of business cards on a table and left.

"Hey, we're having some fun now!" Pacey exclaimed. "All righty then, as the loser was saying, let's plan this puppy."

An hour later, the logistics for the Teen Celeb-For-A-Day Auction were set, and the meeting broke up.

Dawson walked over to Joey before she could escape. "I was surprised to see you here."

"I don't know why," Joey said stiffly. "I'm the one who actually cares about the lighthouse, remember?"

"I also remember how much you hate meetings. Or joining in. Or voluntarily walking into Capeside High, for that matter."

"Well, maybe you don't know me as well as you think you do, Dawson." She turned to go, but he put his hand on her arm. She looked at him, but her eyes were cold.

"Maybe I know you even better than you know yourself," he said quietly.

Joey's lip curled in a nasty smile. "And maybe you don't know me at all anymore, Dawson, so just stop presuming that you do and we'll both be better off."

She walked away. He was helpless. All he could do was stand there and watch her go.

"Having a *Casablanca* moment?" Jen asked as she walked over with Jack.

"She's the one who revels in sad love stories," Dawson said, as Joey exited out the rear doors. "I'm the sorry fool who still believes in happy endings."

Jen linked her arm through his. "Hang in there,

Dawson. When it comes to you and Joey, the movie is definitely not over yet."

Pacey bounded over to them. "Okay, so except for Bitsy Bannerman turning into the Antichrist in a miniskirt, I thought that went really well, didn't you?"

Jack looked at him contemplatively. "I have to tell you, Pacey, I was surprised when I found out you were the one who started this thing."

"If you'd known him as long as I have, that surprise would register more on the level of mind-boggling shock," Dawson said.

"Where's the good ol' Pacey who took pride in his slothful slackerhood?" Jen teased.

"There's Pacey BA and Pacey AA," Pacey explained.

They looked at him blankly. "AA?" Jack finally asked. "Pacey, I had no idea that—"

"Caring about the lighthouse, getting this fund-raiser going, that isn't me and everyone knows it," Pacey said.

"But you just did it," Jack pointed out.

Pacey smiled. "Not me, my man. I thought for sure you'd get it. Who has the most take-charge and do-something positive energy of anyone we know? Who could never stand by and let injustice happen without fighting for what's right?"

One by one they smiled, as the answer came to them.

"BA—Before Andie," Jen played translator. "AA—"

"Exactly," Pacey filled in. "And she's not here to do it, so . . ." He shrugged. "Amazing. She's a pain in the butt all the way from Providence. And she has a hell of a lot of nerve turning me into such a disgustingly productive citizen."

"She'll be really proud of you for doing this, Pacey," Dawson assured him.

"Well, you know what they say," Pacey began. "Behind every great man is a great woman. And behind every great woman is a great behind. And damn, but I miss hers."

# Chapter 3

"**A**re you sure you want to put yourself through this?" Bessie, Joey's older sister, asked as she rocked her young son, Alexander, in her arms. Joey stood in front of the cracked mirror in their tiny hallway trying to get her hair into a French twist.

"Our budget is sure," Joey mumbled through the bobby pins in her mouth. "The Bannermans are paying a mint." She glanced down at the typed sheet on the table, provided by Barbi Bannerman:

**Information Sheet for Serving Staff for
Summer Lights Cocktail Party**

1. All servers must wear well-fitted black tuxedoes, male and female. Rental information can be found below.
2. Cosmetics should be kept to a tasteful

minimum. All female servers with hair longer than chin-length must style it in a French twist or bun, no stray tendrils, please.

3. All servers shall not, under any circumstances, engage in conversation with the invited guests, nor peruse the offerings at the silent auction, nor engage in any other activity other than their professional responsibilities.

The list went on from there, down to rules for nails (clear or pale polish only, nails trimmed), shoes (black, well polished), and even demeanor (pleasantly smiling at all times, helpful to each and every guest).

"You think it's okay to go to the bathroom?" Joey mumbled to herself. "Or is that against the law, too, Mrs. Bannerman?"

"You want some help with that?" Bessie offered, as Joey's French twist came apart again.

"Forget it, I'll stick it into a bun. Clearly I'm not the sophisticated, French-twist type." Joey twirled her hair around at the nape of her neck and stabbed it in place with a couple of pins. She smoothed down the bottom of her tux jacket, rented from Capeside Formals for the occasion.

"Well?"

"You look darling," Bessie assured her.

"Right. I look like a tall girl in drag."

"I swear to you, Joey, you look cuter in a tux than most girls look in some expensive evening gowns."

Joey kissed her cheek. "You're so sweet when you lie, Bessie." She grabbed her tattered backpack off the couch and slung it over one shoulder. "Well, here I go. Off to serve the idle rich. I just keep telling myself it's for a good cause."

Bessie nodded. "Yeah. Saving the lighthouse is cool."

"I was thinking more along the lines of paying our electric bill," Joey said. "Catch ya later."

"Welcome aboard the *Itsy Bitsy*," Barbi Bannerman told Dawson, Pacey, and Jen, showing off perfectly capped teeth.

They had just boarded the Bannermans' yacht—that appeared to be roughly the size of a floating version of the White House—by crossing a metal gangway covered by a red velvet carpet strewn with rose petals and flanked by two liveried butlers, both of whom managed to keep a straight face.

Dawson and Pacey had both rented tuxedos. Dawson had also rented hideous black patent-leather shoes that the guy at Capeside Formals insisted had to be worn with a tux.

Regarding the shoes, Pacey flatly refused, and proudly wore his Doc Martens boots. He had added bright red socks and had thrown a matching red silk scarf around his neck for that added dash of color. Serious movie-star-type sunglasses completed his look.

Jen had called home and had one of her evening gowns sent by FedEx to her. As much as she had loathed dressing formally when she lived in New York—because her mother insisted that she be appropriately clad for the opera, or the ballet, or whatever—it was kind of fun to be wearing an evening gown in Capeside, she'd decided.

*"Itsy Bitsy,"* Pacey mused, all mock earnestness. "Let me take a wild guess—you named it after your charming daughter? And the Itsy thing—*love* the irony!"

Barbi laughed. "It is cute, isn't it. Unfortunately, Bitsy isn't here this evening. One of her friends from boarding school invited her to Paris for the weekend."

*So much for Bitsy's dedication to the cause,* Jen thought wryly. *And we'll all miss her so. And she'll never get to see that Dawson and Pacey really are Screenplay Videos!*

"Let's go over a few things, shall we?" Barbi asked. Then she went on and on about exactly what she expected of the "professional videographer" from Screenplay Videos.

Jen simply tuned her out.

*Barbi Bannerman is a variation on a very boring theme,* Jen thought, studying her with amusement. *Middle-aged socialite clone. Perfectly groomed. Hair oh-so-tastefully streaked. Already booked for her face-lift. Jewelry that could put Dawson and Pacey through the college of their choice.*

*Beyond boring. Bitsy in twenty-five years.*

Barbi took them on a quick tour of the yacht. A tuxedoed pianist played standards on a grand piano as an orchestra was setting up on the mammoth deck. A glittering sign that read "Save Dunn's Lighthouse" hung on one wall, with a painting of the lighthouse illuminated by giant spotlights. Caterers were busily putting the finishing touches on the buffet and the bartenders were setting up the bar. At the opposite end, a blond woman supervised the place cards on the silent auction tables. The entire yacht was strung with tiny, twinkly lights.

Jen was proud of how she'd pulled off getting this gig for Dawson. She'd simply pulled a few strings on her father's side of the family (the ones who didn't see her enough to know about her scandalous rep) and had gotten various society types to call Barbi Bannerman to say that Screenplay Videos was an absolute must to video her fund-raiser.

*And it worked,* Jen thought, smirking. *Honestly, these society wannabe types are the easiest marks in the world.*

"Mr. Leery, if you could just try to catch the guests in a casual, natural way as they board the yacht," Barbi Bannerman said.

"Fine," Dawson replied. "Please call me Dawson."

"Dawson." Barbi nodded. "And please be as unobtrusive as possible during the evening," she went on, "though it's imperative that you get video on each and every guest so that no one feels slighted."

"No chance of that, Ms. Bannerman," Pacey assured her. "I'm Pacey Witter, by the way. Do call me Pacey." He flung the end of his red silk scarf over one shoulder, then raised his sunglasses to give her a Tom Cruise–like smile.

Barbi smiled back uncertainly. "Uh, you came highly recommended by some very important people in New York who know your work, but I have to say you are very young."

Pacey put one arm chummily around her shoulder. "Barbi—might I call you Barbi? Surely a woman of your beauty, breeding, and obvious youth understands that today true artistic genius, such as that possessed by those of us at Screenplay Videos, is not a function of age."

"Well, I—" Barbi began.

"Barbi, Barbi, Barbi," Pacey chided her. He crossed one ankle over the other just as Barbi glanced down and took in his boots and bright red socks.

She gasped. "What is *that?*"

Pacey looked down, raising one leg of his tux pants.

"The youthful artistic expression of genius in its formative stages."

"But I specifically handed out an apparel guide—"

"Barbi, as one artist to another," Pacey began, "surely you understand that youthful genius must not be stifled. Would you have stopped Shakespeare from penning *Romeo and Juliet* because of the color of his *socks?*"

"I, er, see your point," Barbi agreed dubiously. She turned to Dawson. "Do ask my guests how they feel about Dunn's Lighthouse, testimonials, that sort of thing."

"That will be my job, Ms. Bannerman," Jen said.

"Delightful," Barbi exclaimed. "I can tell that you'll fit right in. I love your gown. Whose is it?"

"Vera Wang," Jen replied. "Love your Ralph Lauren, by the way. And the jewelry—Harry Winston?"

"Why, yes." Barbi was clearly relieved that Jen was of her class. "What was your name again, dear?"

"Jennifer Lindley. Of the New York Lindleys. I

think you know my Aunt Martha from the New York City Ballet board?"

"Oh, yes. Wonderful woman. We keep a place in the city, you know. My husband and I spend a great deal of time there. Well, I'll just go see to the serving staff. Let me know if you need anything at all. Oh, lovely that you're here helping with our event, Jennifer."

Jennifer smiled demurely, and she, Pacey, and Dawson all gave Barbi reassuring little waves as she hurried off.

"That would be Jennifer Lindley of the brazen hussy Lindleys," Pacey sniffed.

"The *New York* brazen hussy Lindleys," Jen corrected.

"We are forever grateful that your pedigree has reassured our hostess," Pacey said, bowing.

Dawson looked around the yacht. "Welcome to the world of the rich and pretentious."

"Not to mention ostentatious," Jen added.

"How do you apply for that job, exactly?" Pacey asked.

Dawson checked the viewfinder on his camera. "A young artistic genius such as yourself will clearly be making his young-artistic-genius fortune in the very near future."

"That's how I see it," Pacey agreed expansively.

"And by the way, Mr. Young-Artist-Genius," Jen added, "Shakespeare wrote *Romeo and Juliet* when he was about thirty."

The orchestra began to play "Come to the Cabaret" from the musical *Cabaret*, as a line of well-dressed people began to cross the flower-strewn red carpet onto the yacht.

"Looks like the guests are starting to walk the plank," Dawson said. "That's our cue."

"We're with you, my man," Pacey said. "And as long as this isn't the *Titanic*, it's time for Screenplay Videos to call 'Action!' "

The Bannermans' party was underway.

# Chapter 4

"They must be offered while they are still hot, Miss Potter," Mr. Goulet admonished Joey, as he placed a large tray of hors d'oeuvres into her hands. "And be sure to identify each one."

"Yes, Mr. Goulet," Joey said.

"Joey, I saw you earlier with Dr. and Mrs. London-Bowers, and you did not identify the dilled shrimp or the curried lamb niblets. That is simply unacceptable behavior at one of my affairs."

"Sorry—" Joey mumbled, balancing the heavy tray on her flattened palm as Mr. Goulet had instructed them.

"And as soon as that tray is empty, come right back here for a refill. The food must keep coming and coming and coming, smoothly, without interruptions. And do something about the hair that has escaped your sloppily assembled bun," he added with distaste.

Joey had to bite her lip to keep from telling Mr. Goulet exactly where he could stuff his curried lamb niblets. She knew for a fact that his real name was Ray Gullet and not Raymond Goulet—pronounced Goo-lay. Because he'd gone to Capeside High School with Bessie before he'd dropped out.

*He was known then for not taking a lot of showers,* Joey thought, recalling the jokes Bessie and her friends used to make about him. She sniffed the air and almost choked.

*And I suspect the latter is still true now.*

When Raymond had selected her as one of the staff who would wander through the crowd offering hot hors d'oeuvres to the guests, she'd been anything but pleased. If only she'd been assigned to the galley or even if she'd been behind the buffet table, she might have been able to avoid Dawson, Pacey, and Jen altogether.

But on the main deck of the vessel, forget it.

Still, so far, they hadn't spotted her. But every time she saw them videoing anywhere near her, she scurried away to offer her tray of food to any group she could spot on the other side of the yacht.

It was weird and horrible and sad to be avoiding Dawson. He was the person she had always been able to go to, to tell the truth to, to—

*No,* Joey told herself firmly. *That was then. This is now. I can't undo what happened or forget what he did.*

As the orchestra segued into an Andrew Lloyd Webber medley, she nodded politely to Raymond, hoisted her tray, and headed into the throng.

*Joey Potter, forever serving other people food,* she thought glumly. *My lot in life.*

"Would you like some?" Joey approached the small group standing near the painting of Dunn's Lighthouse. "Dilled shrimp, warm duck pâté on toast points, puff pastry stuffed with Brie and mushrooms, curried lamb niblets."

It was amazing how much food rich people could eat when the food was free. The crowd gathered around her, swiftly gobbling up every morsel. Within minutes her tray was empty again. She knew she should hurry right back to the galley for a new trayful of hors d'oeuvres, so it could keep coming and coming and coming, but she hadn't had a real break since she'd started work two hours earlier, and she definitely needed to use the bathroom.

Joey dropped off her tray in the kitchen, grabbed her backpack, and headed to a lower deck, where a sign that read "Ladies Who Love Dunn's Lighthouse" had been hung outside the largest rest room.

She went in.

At the moment, anyway, no other Dunn's Lighthouse–loving ladies were inside. She used the toilet in privacy, washed at one of the ornate marble sinks, then sank into a comfortable chair and sighed with relief.

Ah. Peace and quiet. Although undoubtedly that affected wanker Gullet would be screeching his head off any minute at her absence. Which meant she had to do something or other to make her hair neater and get her butt back to the main deck.

She opened her backpack to take out her brush and noticed that her sketch pad was still there. Impulsively, she took it out and flipped it open to her drawing of Quinn, the one she'd been working on when Dawson and Jen had showed up.

She regarded it carefully. So many hours working on it already, and still it wasn't quite right. People were so much tougher to capture than things. So much more complicated than just light and shadow.

She flipped the pages of the book to a series of four sketches of Dunn's Lighthouse, each done in a different light.

Much better. She especially liked the one she'd done at dawn, just as the fog was clearing and the edges of everything were—

"Joey?"

She looked up. Jen.

"Surprise," Joey said, her voice flat.

Jen took in Joey's outfit. "You're working?"

"Actually, I'm here to bid on the Concorde flight and weekend in London."

"Okay, that was a stupid question," Jen admitted. "I just meant I'm surprised I haven't run into you all night if we're both working here."

"It's called avoidance. I'm very good at it."

"Avoiding Dawson, you mean."

"Excellent deductive powers." Joey got up. "You'll have to excuse me, Jen, the hired help aren't allowed to mingle. It was on our instruction sheet."

"Get off it, Joey. I'm hired help, too, remember? You think I care about all this pretentious crap?"

"I find it highly amusing when pretentious crap professes not to care about pretentious crap," Joey replied smoothly.

Jen folded her arms. "I don't deserve that."

Joey sighed. "Ignore me. It's the infamous Joey Potter defense mechanism kicking in." She caught sight of her reflection in the bank of lit mirrors, and sighed wearily. "I'm supposed to paste these flyaway hairs to my head before I return to serve the huddled and bejeweled masses. Though how I'm supposed to accomplish that remains a mystery."

"Style-fix," Jen pronounced.

Joey gave her a sarcastic look. "Gee, I meant to pick some up."

Jen reached into her tiny evening bag and pulled out a tiny jar. "Miss Jen's House o' Beauty is now open for business. Sit over there."

It was an order, not a request. Joey sat on one of the pink silk–covered stools in front of the mirrors as Jen deftly applied the hair product to Joey's hair and smoothed it back.

"Done," Jen pronounced. "Sleek and shiny."

"Thanks. Really. And I'm sorry about before."

Jen smiled at Joey's reflection in the mirror. "You're welcome. Really. And forget about before." She dropped the Style-fix back into her purse.

Joey got up. "Well, duty calls."

"Joey, feel free to say this is none of my business, but avoiding Dawson isn't the answer to—"

"It's none of your business," Joey interrupted. "Look, I don't expect you to understand. The complexity of my relationship with Dawson is not something that can be explained away in some well-written, two-line movie moment. There's no script for this."

"There's no script for any of it, Joey. It's all messy

and complicated and scary as hell. You're not the only one."

"Wait, is this the part where we get all deep and profound and bond like sisters?" Joey asked. "Because I really hate that." She went to get her backpack. "Thanks for the—"

"Wait, you forgot something." Jen picked up Joey's sketch pad and stared at the drawing of Dunn's Lighthouse. "You did this?"

"It's not done," Joey said quickly.

"This is great, Joey. I mean it."

"Please, it is nowhere near the vicinity of 'great.' "

"I know how much compliments pain you," Jen said dryly, "especially from me. So how about 'better than very good'?"

"I'll settle for 'decent for a rank amateur.' "

Jen eyed her. "You've got talent. You can believe me, or not. It's not like I have any reason to flatter you. And frankly, the small-town-chick-who-doesn't-know-who-she-really-is thing is getting kind of tired, so get over it."

"How delightfully self-help of you," Joey quipped.

"Come on, Joey, all I'm saying is—"

"Why, it's Dunn's Lighthouse!" a loud voice exclaimed.

Two older women had come into the rest room, but Joey and Jen had been too involved to notice. Now they stood by Jen, peering at Joey's drawing.

Red-faced, Joey grabbed the sketch book from Jen.

"Are you the artist, my dear?" the older of the two women asked Joey.

"It's just a sketch," Joey mumbled, stuffing the book into her backpack.

"Take that out this instant!" the older woman commanded. Joey was so taken aback that she actually did it. The woman held out her hand. Joey handed over her sketch pad.

"Excellent. Isn't it, Elsa?" She held it up to the other woman.

The other woman nodded. "Lovely."

The gray-haired woman looked at Joey. "And you are?"

"Joey Potter. But the drawing isn't—"

"Potter, Potter . . . familiar name . . ." The light dawned. "Wasn't it your father who—"

"Excuse me, I have to get back to work." Joey held her hand out for her sketch pad.

"Oh nonsense, young lady. I don't care who your father is or what he did. I'm dealing with you. I'm Patricia Axworthy, this is my sister, Elsa. She's younger, I'm richer, which allows me to be as obnoxious as I want to be. Now, then. What do you charge to purchase this work?"

Joey's jaw fell open. This woman was actually offering to *buy* her sketch? As in pay *money* for it?

"A lot," Jen filled in, since Joey seemed unable to speak. "I'm her agent."

"I know exactly who you are, dear," the older woman said. "Your Aunt Martha is a friendly enemy of mine, and someone pointed you out to me on the street one day. And believe me, you're the only one in your family with any balls." She turned back to Joey. "Name your price."

This time Joey reached for her sketch pad and

firmly took it out of Patricia Axworthy's hands. "It's not for sale."

"Don't be ridiculous. I'm sure you need the money."

Joey's jaw set hard. *I'll eat dirt before I grovel in front of you,* she thought.

"Thank you for the offer, Mrs. Axworthy. But this work is not for sale."

"Unless you were planning to buy it and then offer it at the blind auction, that is," Jen added quickly.

Joey shot her a scathing look.

"She only sells her work for charities she believes in," Jen explained.

"Excellent notion," Mrs. Axworthy said, opening her purse. "I shall write you a check, my dear. Then I'll take this piece up to the auction. You will be able to say you did your part to help save Dunn's Lighthouse."

Joey nodded. She couldn't very well turn that down.

The older woman scribbled something on the check, folded it in half, and handed it to Joey. Joey carefully tore her sketch out of her book and handed it over. And the Axworthy sisters sailed out of the rest room.

"Did that really just happen?" Joey asked.

"It did," Jen confirmed. "Aren't you going to look at how much she paid you?"

Joey unfolded the check, amazed. "Seventy-five dollars!"

Jen smiled. "Whoever bids the most for the sketch

is getting a bargain, no matter what they pay. They'll have a Joey Potter original from her early period."

Joey shoved her sketch pad and the check into her backpack. "Why do I feel like in the movie version of our lives, you get played by Gwyneth at her most genteel, and I get played by Christina Ricci in *The Opposite of Sex?*"

Jen laughed. "Frankly, I'm much more the Christina type. And damn proud of it."

"Well, Mr. Goulet Gourmet is probably sweating dilled shrimp over my extended absence." Joey fingered the strap of her backpack. "I believe my next line should be 'thank-you.'"

"And I believe mine is 'you're welcome.' Are you coming to the Teen Celeb Auction tomorrow?"

Joey nodded. "Now that I'm rich with a whole seventy-five dollars, maybe I'll even bid on someone." She headed for the door, stopped, and looked back. "Jen, tell Dawson that I—"

"Whatever it is, why don't you tell him yourself?"

Joey knew the answer, but it wasn't something she could explain. Not to Jen, anyway. As far as Joey could see, Jen never tripped over her own heart.

So there was really nothing to say at all.

# Chapter 5

"Hiding in the bathroom is so not Jen Lindley," Jack called to Jen.

"I'm not hiding. I'm primping," Jen called back.

Jack, who was sitting on Jen's bed, checked his watch. "If you don't get out here soon, the Celeb Auction will be over before we get there."

"Okay, if I look like an idiot, you have to promise to tell me the truth," Jen called.

"You look like an idiot," Jack called back.

Jen laughed. "Watch it, or I'll start a rumor that you're gay."

Jack smiled. At least he *could* smile about it now. Sometimes, at least.

Jen walked out of the bathroom. She was wearing a shocking pink circle skirt with a red poodle on it, and a puffy-sleeved white blouse covered in huge pink, red, yellow, and royal blue polka dots. Her hair was held back by tiny multicolored barrettes. Her lipstick was the same hot pink as her skirt, and it matched the pink portion of her pink-and-white saddle shoes.

Jack stared at her blankly.

"You don't get it?" Jen asked.

"You're someone with very bad taste?" Jack ventured.

"Nice try. Reese Witherspoon in *Pleasantville*. She goes through the TV and ends up living in a fifties TV show? And everything is in black and white except her because she's having sex?"

Jack shrugged. "I never saw the movie."

"Movie deprivation is a sad state, Jack. One which we'll rectify in a marathon rental session sometime soon." Jen looked him over. "Let me guess. You're dressed as some dark, brooding, sensitive type."

"I'm not in costume, Jen."

"Duh, Jack. I just wish you'd change your mind and join in the fun and games."

"Okay, you convinced me. Just let me throw on one of your frocks and I'll can do Nathan Lane from *The Birdcage*. A movie I actually saw. No one would expect that from me, huh?"

She sat next to him on her bed and playfully bumped her shoulder against his. "Hey, have I mentioned lately how much I like having you living here with me and Grams?"

"When you asked me to move in, you're the one who did me the favor, Jen."

She shook her head. "Trust me. My head was getting really . . . I'm just glad you're here. And I'm

48

glad you're my friend. Even if I couldn't convince you to dress as Charlton Heston doing Moses in *The Ten Commandments*. Ever notice how much eyeliner he wore in that flick?"

"Never saw it," Jack said.

"Jack, Jack, Jack. We may have to dedicate the entire next month to Remedial Film 101. And there will be a final exam." She pulled him up off the bed, and they headed for the door.

Jack caught sight of a photo tucked into the edge of Jen's mirror showing Jen, Dawson, Pacey, Joey, and Andie fooling around on the beach. He'd been the photographer. Pacey's arms were wrapped around Andie, and she looked so happy.

"Know what I miss more than bad films, Jen?"

Jen looked over at the photo too. "Not 'what' but 'who.' Right?"

Jack nodded. "At the moment, even my sister's most annoying habits fill me with a certain nostalgia."

"She'll be back, Jack. You'll see."

"I hope so. But we dark, brooding types tend to think of positive thinking as wishful thinking."

At the docks, where the Celeb Auction was set to start at ten in the morning, the sun was already hot and Lauryn Hill hip-hop grooves blasted from a kick-butt sound system.

Dawson wore a T-shirt that read "What I Really Want to Do Is Direct." He'd already been there for over an hour, setting up his equipment on a small platform just outside the thick of the crowd. The platform had been assembled early that morning by a dozen volunteers. They'd also built a makeshift stage where Pacey stood in the middle of a group of people, deep in conversation.

A huge banner hung over the stage that read "Teens! Make a Teen Celeb Yours for the Day! Save Dunn's Lighthouse!" Someone had tried to draw the lighthouse on the banner, complete with Quinn in the upper window, but it looked more like Rapunzel in a watchtower.

Dawson looked over the huge crowd, clearly in a party mood. Impressive. Evidently Pacey's hard work had paid off. There had been an article in the local newspaper, coverage on TV, and endless signs plastered all over town. Enterprising food vendors were selling everything from cotton candy to popcorn to slush cones.

Two teens were even hawking T-shirts silkscreened with a photo of Quinn sitting in Dunn's Lighthouse that read "Quinn's In Until We Win. Save Dunn's Lighthouse, Capeside, Mass." They were selling for twenty bucks a pop and doing a brisk business.

For a moment, a girl with her back to him looked just like Joey, her long chestnut brown hair glinting in the morning sunlight. She turned around, laughing about something.

Not Joey.

*She might show up and she might not*, Dawson told himself. *There's no point in thinking about it, because even if she does show up, she's not getting up close and personal with you. Not as your girlfriend, that's for sure. And not even as your friend. Not now.*

*Maybe not ever.*

That thought filled him with a kind of pain akin to a lifetime of root canal minus the novocaine. So it just couldn't be so. Some things were simply impossible, like seeing *Citizen Kane* too many times, having the artists at Capeside High valued as much as the jocks, or losing Joey forever.

"Hey, Dawson," Jen called as she and Jack ambled over to him. "Big crowd, huh?"

"Impressive," Dawson agreed. "But then, excitement in Capeside can be hard to come by. You look great, Jen. *Pleasantville*, right?"

She grinned. "I knew I could count on you, Dawson. And before you ask: no, Jack isn't in costume."

"I'm simply an observer at this event," Jack explained.

Jen eyed him thoughtfully. "Because you were afraid no one would bid on you?"

"Blunt is her middle name," Dawson said.

"Well?" Jen asked.

Jack nodded. "There's probably some truth to that. But also because the idea of dressing as a celebrity and doing someone's bidding all day sounds horrifying."

"You just won the title of Assistant to the Videographer," Dawson said. He threw Jack a notebook and a pen. "When the auction starts, write down the celebrity's real name, celebrity name, who won him or her, and how much the final bid is. Oh yeah. Where they're going and what they're doing."

"We haven't discussed salary," Jack said, but he scribbled down what Dawson had just said.

"Same as mine," Dawson replied. He squinted through his viewfinder. "So, has anyone seen Joey?"

"Not that you care," Jen added. She couldn't help herself. The green-headed monster welled up every time she was reminded that Dawson's heart would always belong to Joey, whether Joey wanted him or not.

Whether Jen wanted him or not.

"It's not exactly news that I care about her, Jen," Dawson said. "For me to deny a deep-rooted concern about her well-being would be hypocritical and futile. And an obvious lie."

Jen rolled her eyes. "Chill, Dawson, I haven't seen her."

*Since last night,* she added mentally. Amazing as it seemed, Dawson and Joey had actually managed to miss each other on board the *Itsy Bitsy* the night before. Dawson was constantly busy videoing. And Joey was careful to stay far away from him.

*Which means he doesn't even know that she sold her drawing of the lighthouse,* Jen thought. *Or whether or not anyone bid on it at the blind auction. I don't even know if anyone bid on it, come to think of it.*

Jen hadn't even mentioned to Jack that Joey had waitressed at the Bannermans' fund-raiser, and she was pretty sure Joey hadn't told him—or anyone else—herself.

*Which means Joey's big triumph of selling a drawing for the very first time remains an unknown. And Joey is not likely to toot her own horn. Trust me to do something nice and then wreck it with a really bitchy follow-up,* Jen thought guiltily.

Chris Wolfe, in the guise of young Elvis Presley, sidled up to Jen. He wore a black ducktail wig and fake sideburns, jeans, a rayon sports shirt with the sleeves rolled, and blue suede shoes. "How's it goin', pretty momma?" he asked in his best Elvis voice.

"Elvis, right?" Jack asked.

"Thank you," Chris replied in his Elvis voice, curling the corner of his lip. "Thank you very much."

"Did you know Elvis was impotent?" Jen asked.

Chris wrapped an arm around Jen's shoulders, dropping the Elvis persona. "But in this case, you know better."

Jen removed his arm and dropped it like a dead carp. "I can't seem to recall all the *little* details. Excuse me, I'm gonna go see if Pacey needs any help. Oh, Chris, you might want to bribe someone to bid on you. Just to avoid the humiliation of the utterly unwanted."

As Jen made her way to the stage, Pacey crossed to the microphone. He was clad in cuffed jeans and a white T-shirt, and his hair was gelled back like James Dean in *Rebel Without a Cause.* "Yo, off the tunes!" he yelled.

Someone complied, and the music ended abruptly. Pacey looked over at Jen, who stood to the side of the stage with an uncostumed Emily LaPaz. He gave Jen a big thumbs-up sign, and she gave it back.

"He's an interesting guy," Emily mused.

"More than meets the eyes," Jen replied.

"Good morning, Capeside!" Pacey boomed into the microphone. He grinned at the audience. "I'm James Dean. Also, unfortunately, known as Pacey Witter. Welcome to the Teen Celebrity Auction to save Dunn's Lighthouse."

The crowd applauded, some even whistled and cheered.

"I'd like to thank Sheriff Witter for the permit we needed to hold this fund-raiser here on the docks. And I'd like to thank everyone who worked so hard the past few days to put this thing together."

"And Quinn!" someone yelled. "Quinn rocks!"

"And Quinn Bickfee," Pacey added. "The Lighthouse Girl hangs in there longer than the Eveready Bunny."

"Bigfoot sucks!" a deep voice bellowed. Heads turned. A small group of angry-looking guys stood just apart from the crowd.

"Yeah, I said it," a barrel-chested guy in a Dale Earnhardt NASCAR T-shirt said belligerently. "She ain't even from Capeside."

Dawson turned his camera on them, zooming in on their livid faces.

"Tear down the damn lighthouse and put up the mall, is what I say," the skinny guy next to him yelled. "We need the work! How many people does the damn lighthouse employ?"

"Try to get their names," Dawson told Jack.

"No thanks," Jack said. "I value my life."

"I respect your position," Pacey said into the microphone. "Maybe we can arrange a debate on the issue sometime soon, where everyone can express their view. But right now we have a permit to be here."

"It's a free country!" the biggest guy challenged. "You can't make us leave."

"But I can," Sheriff Witter said, coming up to the group of hecklers, his son Deputy Doug by his side. "You can break this up peaceably, or not. It's your call."

The biggest guy cursed under his breath. "Let's get the hell out of here," he told his friends. He stabbed a finger toward Pacey up on stage. "This ain't over, you little twerp!"

"That's Mr. Little Twerp to you," Pacey replied into the mike, and everyone laughed; the tension broke as the rabble-rousers walked away.

"So here's how the auction works," Pacey explained. "Teens dressed as celebs will come up here and any teen can make an offer for them. The bidding will keep going, and the highest bidder wins the celeb for the afternoon."

"Only teens?" a grandfather-type clad in a Quinn T-shirt called out jovially.

"Yep," Pacey replied. "Sorry, it's a teen thing." He looked down at his clipboard. "All righty, then. First up for auction is Xena, the Warrior Princess."

All six feet of Gaelynn Tucci, captain of Capeside High's girls' basketball team, bounded up onstage in her Xena outfit. She struck a muscle pose to applause and good-natured whistles.

"The bidding will start at ten bucks," Pacey said.

"Twelve!" a guy from Pacey's English class yelled.

"Fifteen!" a short freshman with a red buzzcut called out.

"Twenty!"

"Twenty from the guy down front in the *Animal House* T-shirt," Pacey repeated. "Do I hear twenty-five?"

"Come on, you can do better than that!" Xena bellowed.

"Twenty-two fifty is all I got!" the freshman buzz-cut called out.

"Going once, going twice . . . Xena is yours for the day at twenty-two fifty!" Pacey cried.

"Yes!" the kid screamed, pumping his fist in the air.

And so it went.

Buffy, Scary Spice, Tori Spelling, Drew Barrymore, and Marilyn Monroe were auctioned off. So was Leonardo, early Michael Jackson, and Tom Cruise in *Risky Business* (clad only in BVDs, white socks, and sunglasses).

The crowd cracked up, hooting and hollering.

"I can't decide if all this is stupid and sexist or mildly amusing in a sophomoric kind of way," Emily LaPaz said to Jen.

Jen shrugged. "Both. Frankly, I decided to leave my depth at home today."

Chris Wolfe as Elvis went to Heather Phillips, a girl he had wooed, won, and dropped within forty-eight hours. While the bidding was still ongoing, she insisted that he get down on one knee and sing "Love Me Tender" to her, over and over.

Eventually, the bidding got around to Jen. She approached the microphone and smiled at the crowd, but a sudden burst of insecurity came over her.

*What if no one bids on me?* she worried. *I should have taken the advice I gave Chris and made a deal with Jack, just in case. I could pay him back whatever he bid.*

Pacey went into his spiel about Jen, also known as Reese Witherspoon in *Pleasantville*.

"Yeah, but does she put out like the girl did in the flick?" Brett Ardor yelled. He was a jocked-out butthole with the redeeming qualities of toenail fungus.

No way was he getting the best of Jen. She lowered her mouth to the microphone. "If I did, you couldn't afford me," she said.

"Ha! Dissed you!" Brett's friend crowed, and everyone laughed.

The bidding started at fifteen bucks, bid by senior Chuck Owens, the three-hundred-pound defensive left end from the Capeside football team. At an end-of-the-school-year party at Chris Wolfe's, he'd guzzled a six-pack and ingested an entire large pepperoni pizza in under five minutes, then lost it all in Chris's swimming pool.

It earned him the nickname Upchuck.

"Okay, we've got a bid of twenty from Upchuck," Pacey said. "Come on, guys, you don't wanna force this beauty to spend the day fetching barf bags, do you? Do I hear twenty-two?"

"Twenty-two," Mark Cabberus, a quiet guy from Jen's English class, called out.

Jen smiled at him. *Hmmm, Mark Cabberus.*

*Smart. Nice. On the right side of decent-looking. Could be interesting . . .*

"Twenty-five!" Chris Wolfe called out from his position on one knee, still singing to Heather.

"Yo, Elvis, you're mine for the day," Heather reminded him. "So let's see those hips swivel in this direction."

"Sorry, Bid Boy, you're out of it," Pacey told him. "Do I hear—"

"Twenty-six!" Upchuck yelled around a half-eaten hot dog he was stuffing in his mouth.

*Gross,* Jen thought. And his hairy stomach stuck out from the bottom of his T-shirt. He turned to say something to someone, and Jen was treated to the rear view. Ugh. His sweat pants were falling below his massive belly, and clearly no one had told him to say no to crack.

"Twenty-eight!" Mark countered.

"Up-chuck! Up-chuck! Up-chuck!" his friend chanted, egging him on, as Upchuck downed the rest of his hot dog in one bite.

"Thirty dollars and that's all I got!" Upchuck yelled, pulling his pockets inside out while his friends cheered.

"Thirty dollars is the bid," Pacey said. He looked over at Mark. "You're not gonna let this woman spend the day with the Upchucker, are you?"

Jen sent him a pleading look, but he just shrugged regretfully.

Out in the crowd, Upchuck leered at her, belched, and scratched parts of his anatomy known only to his proctologist.

"The bid is thirty dollars," Pacey repeated. "Going once, going twice . . ."

Jen frantically tried to make eye contact with Jack, but he was busy writing something down and didn't notice.

Pacey turned to Jen. "Those of us who know the sacrifice you are about to make for Capeside salute you. Going, going—"

"Fifty dollars!" a male voice rang out from the back of the crowd.

Exclamations of surprise rumbled through the crowd, as people craned their necks to see who had just made the bid.

He was leaning against a tree. Medium tall. Dark hair. Sinewy athletic body in khakis and a loose shirt over a T-shirt. Movie-star handsome behind dark sunglasses.

"Who is he?" people whispered to each other. No one recognized him.

"Fifty dollars from tall, dark, and mysterious in the back," Pacey announced.

"Hurry up and end it," Jen hissed to Pacey, lest Upchuck's friends decide to chip in so he could overbid.

"Going once, going twice, gone to the guy leaning against the—"

"Hey, hold up!" Upchuck bellowed. "We don't know him. How do we even know he's a teen?"

Pacey scratched his chin. "Interesting query, Upchuck. Look at it this way. Do we not accept on faith that you are, in fact, human? Or do we demand proof?"

Upchuck opened his mouth to answer.

"Consider that rhetorical," Pacey said quickly. "Sold to the guy in the back for fifty big ones."

*Thank God,* Jen thought, as she hurried off the stage. A day with Upchuck would have been a day of agony. Whereas the gorgeous stranger who had bid fifty dollars for her looked as if he could be very, very interesting, indeed.

"I think we're done with all the celebs, except me," Pacey said. "James Dean, the original rebel without a—"

"Hey, you forgot me!" Brett Ardor yelled, bounding up to the stage. He was dressed in his Capeside High baseball team uniform, with a sign hanging around his neck that read "Mark McGwire."

Brett pushed Pacey away from the microphone. "Hey, hey, ladies," came his amplified voice. "I'm Mark McGwire."

"Not!" a girl down front yelled.

Brett turned around, wiggling his butt. On the back, his sign read "I Score Cuz My Bat's So Big!" He turned back around and applauded for himself. "Come on, ladies. It's thrill time!"

"Boo!" one girl yelled.

"The only one who wants to swing your bat is you," added another.

"Bidding starts at . . . fifty cents," Pacey decided.

"Hey!" Brett objected over the crowd's laughter.

Pacey shrugged. "I calls 'em like I sees 'em, my man."

"Fifty cents!" Heather yelled.

"But you already have me," Chris pointed out.

"Keep crooning, Elvis, I think I can handle it," Heather sneered.

"Do I hear a bid of fifty-one?" Pacey asked.

There were a few titters, but no bids. Dawson let his camera pan the crowd. Girls were whispering to each other and laughing. Evidently there had been a mass female group decision to let Brett go for the humiliating sum of fifty cents.

"No other bidders for the guy with delusions of bat grandeur?" Pacey asked, as Dawson swung his camera back to the stage. "Going, going—"

"Fifty-one cents."

Dawson swung the camera to the right, from where he'd heard the bidder's voice. Not that he needed physical proof to know who'd just spoken. It was a voice he would recognize anytime, any place, anywhere.

Joey. Standing alone, her arms folded.

Now, Dawson recalled that when pictures of Joey in lingerie had ended up on the Internet, without Joey's knowledge or permission, Brett Ardor had made Joey's life a living hell. He'd made sucking noises every time she walked by. He'd asked the most intimate and embarrassing questions about her body and her sex life, always in front of as many people as possible.

Up on stage, Pacey grinned hugely. He knew what hell Brett had put Joey through, too.

It was payback time.

"Sold to Joey Potter for fifty-one cents," Pacey announced. "Joey, play ball!"

Smirking, Joey crooked one finger at Brett, who

lumbered off the stage as everyone hooted and laughed.

"And now, finally, last, and also least, yours most truly," Pacey said. "And now, my imitation of James Dean in *Giant.*" He cleared his throat.

" 'My well come in, Bick. I'm a rich 'un.' "

Off to the side of the stage, Emily LaPaz applauded.

"Thanks," Pacey said. "Clearly a woman who knows talent when she hears it. So, bidding for me will start at . . . ten cents?" he ventured.

"Five dollars," Uma Sorensen, a foreign exchange student from Sweden, yelled loudly from the crowd.

Pacey went into amazement mode. Yowza. Uma was a flaxen-haired goddess who would look at home in the swimsuit issue of *Sports Illustrated.*

*Not that I'm interested,* Pacey reminded himself. *My heart belongs to Andie. However, the rest of me might find an afternoon with Uma right up there on the fun-o-meter.*

"Ten dollars," Emily LaPaz called out.

Pacey's head swung over to Emily. She of the intellect, the sense of humor, the butt the size of New Jersey. Bidding for him against the beauteous Uma?

"Uh, we have a bid of ten dollars," Pacey said. "Anyone want to go twelve?" Pacey eyed Uma hopefully.

*Bid again, Uma,* Pacey silently urged. *You can do it. I swear I'll refund every penny. I'll pay interest. Interest on interest.*

"Twelve dollars," Uma called.

Clearly, there was a God.

"Twelve dollars," Pacey echoed triumphantly.

"And since I know I'm not worth it, we'll stop right there. Going once, going—"

"Fifteen dollars," Emily called.

"On the other hand, I may have underestimated my studly appeal," Pacey said lamely. "Do I hear a higher bid?"

Silence.

"It wouldn't have to be a lot higher . . ."

Laughter. No bid. The fair Uma, in fact, was busy petting some Joe-college-frat-boy type's cute dog.

"And I am had for fifteen bucks," Pacey said glumly. "Which brings the bidding to a close. Let the fun and games, er, begin."

*Chapter 6*

As the winning bidders got together with their celebrities, the crowd began to thin out. Dawson needed to formulate a schedule to video as many of the celebs and winning bidders as possible.

"Did you get all the matches written down?" he asked Jack, as he gathered up his equipment.

"It wasn't brain surgery, Dawson. However a lot of the winning bidders weren't what you would describe as articulate about where they and their celeb could be located or what they'd be doing."

Jack tore the list he'd made out of the notebook and held it out to Dawson.

But Dawson's attention was elsewhere.

Not far away, Joey stood, leaning against a tree, talking with her celeb-for-a-day, the infamous Brett Ardor.

Purchased by her for fifty-one cents.

"Take a deep breath, Dawson," Jack said. "I don't think Brett is exactly going to steal her heart."

"That reassurance was not necessary, but thanks." Dawson took the list.

"She's not in relationship mode now, Dawson. My advice is that you need to just let her be for a while."

Dawson could feel his temper flare. "You know, Jack, just because you took a chance and masqueraded as her significant other for a while doesn't qualify you as an expert on Joey Potter."

Jack returned Dawson's steely gaze. "And just because you think that you knew her when, don't assume you know her now. People change, Dawson. And unlike the scripts you write, you don't get to manipulate how they change or even why they change. And toughest of all, you don't get to control whether or not the person they become is a person who wants you."

He turned and walked away.

Dawson sighed.

"Where'd Jack go?" Jen asked, walking over to him.

"To nurse the wounds I just inflicted. Why aren't you with . . ." Dawson scanned the list Jack had made. Next to Jen's name was a big question mark. "Who was that guy who bid on you, anyway?"

"Excellent question. It seems my mystery bidder was not really the bidder at all."

"Translated into English, that would be—?"

Jen thrust a folded piece of paper at Dawson. "Mystery Man handed me *this* and took off."

Dawson unfolded the note, which had been typed

on a computer, and read it out loud. " 'To Jen Lindley: The winning bidder for your company this afternoon did not wish to be present at the auction. Please be at the flagpole in front of Capeside High at one o'clock this afternoon.' "

He handed the note back to Jen. "Are you going to do it?"

"Why not? I have to admit it, Dawson. My curiosity has been tweaked."

"Did the safety factor, or lack of safety factor, ever enter your tweaked mind?" Dawson asked. "This note could have been written by anyone from Mark Cabberus to Hannibal Lecter."

"Your concern that I'm not devoured by a cannibalistic, albeit fictitious, serial killer is touching, Dawson."

"All right, so I indulged in some minor hyperbole for dramatic effect. Seriously, Jen, I still don't think you should go alone."

"To the flagpole? In front of the high school? At one o'clock in the afternoon?" Jen laughed. "Sounds real risky to me."

Dawson wasn't laughing.

"Tell you what, why don't you come with me," Jen suggested. "Me discovering my mystery date could be great for your video."

"Deal," Dawson agreed. "I'll go film some of the others and meet you back here at, say, a quarter to one."

Jen nodded. "Deal. I think I'll go find Jack."

"Tell him . . ." Dawson hesitated.

Jen shook her head. "You and Joey deserve each other. You both send messages through me."

"She sent me a message?" Dawson asked, trying hard not to sound too eager.

"The same message you just sent Jack." She smiled wryly, walking away backwards. "And so it goes."

"So, Emily LaPaz," Pacey said too heartily, "imagine you bidding on me." He tried to plaster a sincere smile on his face. They were strolling by the creek, as Emily had suggested.

"Imagine," Emily agreed.

Pacey searched his mind for some topic of conversation. Unsuccessfully. Though they'd gone to school together for years, he really didn't know Emily at all. She was smart, that was for sure, near the top of their class. Though, as Andie had once pointed out to him, Emily was not one of those supercilious types who felt the need to show off her mental prowess. She'd always been perfectly pleasant to him, friendly enough.

Frankly, the only time he'd ever given Emily LaPaz a moment's thought was when he and Dawson had been having an argument about the importance of physical attraction and he'd used Emily as an example.

*"Would you go out with Emily LaPaz?"* Pacey recalled challenging Dawson, who was expounding to him about the importance of inner beauty. *"Nice, smart, butt the size of New Jersey?"*

Now he cast a sideways glance at Emily. Her face was actually kind of pretty. Soft features. Nice brown eyes.

But the rest of her, from the waist down, was rather large. And that was an understatement.

And Pacey had to spend the entire day with her.

"So, Emily, just out of curiosity, why did you bid on me?" Pacey asked, dodging around a kid chasing after a flying Frisbee.

"I could flatter you and tell you that I've had a massive crush on you for years—"

"You have?" Pacey asked, startled.

"No. But I could flatter you and say that." Emily smiled at him sweetly. "Actually, it was purely impetuous. You came as James Dean. I happen to be the world's hugest James Dean fan."

Pacey smiled and nodded. "Wow."

*If only Uma had been a bigger James Dean fan,* Pacey thought wistfully. *I could be strolling along next to a Nordic goddess instead of next to . . . who I'm next to.*

"James Dean grew up in a small town, you know," Emily went on. "In Indiana. Fairmount, actually. I've been there, actually. A lot like Capeside, minus the ocean."

"Uh-huh." It was going to be a very long day.

"It's funny about icons who die young," Emily mused. "It's tragic, of course. But in another way, it's kind of perfect. Because they're forever young and shining, you know? They never grow old. Or disappoint anyone."

"Well, Disappointing is my middle name," Pacey quipped, "so I guess that means I'll live to a ripe old age."

Emily smiled. "Me, too. And here you thought we had nothing in common."

Pacey was taken aback. "I never said we didn't have anything in—"

"Disappointing is only one of my middle names," Emily interrupted. "The other one is Mindreader. Come on, I live just down this block. We're going to my house. My parents are out of town, so no one is home. Lucky, huh?"

"Lucky" was definitely not the first adjective that came to Pacey's mind.

*Chapter 7*

*T*he last thing I want to do is to spend the day with Emily LaPaz, Pacey thought, as she opened the front door to a white house with green trim that looked pretty much like every other middle-class house on the tree-lined middle-class block.

"I'm so glad my parents are out of town," Emily said, leading him into the living room. "Aren't we incredibly lucky?"

*Correction*, Pacey mentally amended. *The last thing I want to do is to spend the day with Emily LaPaz. At her house. Alone with her.*

"Nice house," Pacey said, just because he couldn't think of anything else to say.

She laughed. "If you're fond of decorators who derive their artistic satisfaction from choosing art that color-coordinates perfectly with the Barca-Lounger. When my father realized that a TV remote could be built right into the armrest, he thought he'd found heaven."

Pacey grinned despite himself. "Maybe he should recommend that model to my dad."

"Maybe he already has," Emily quipped. "Hungry? I could make us something to eat. I'm a really good cook."

*Figures,* Pacey thought.

"Oh no, but you go ahead."

She gave him an arch look as she led him into the kitchen, decorated with way too much yellow and white bric-a-brac. "I have to tell you, Pacey, you're not being very James Deanish with me. Hardly the actor I bargained and bid for."

"No?"

"No. More brooding is definitely required." She put out a platter of butterscotch cookies and poured them both glasses of lemonade. "Much more."

"Brooding. I'll have to work on that," Pacey said. They sat on tall stools at a high counter and ate cookies. Pacey ate cookie after cookie, for want of anything better to do.

"So, how long have you been into James Dean?" she asked him, as she reached for still another cookie.

Pacey shrugged. "Dawson and I rented *Rebel Without a Cause* years ago and fell deeply in love with Natalie Wood. And James Dean actually got her, so—"

"Vicarious thrills, huh?" Emily said.

"Exactly," Pacey agreed. "I admit it."

"What about the other movies?" Emily asked, as she nibbled on one of the cookies.

71

"Loved *East of Eden,* liked *Giant,*" Pacey told her.

"Me, too."

"Dean was the epitome of the cool, sensitive, misunderstood rebel," Pacey went on. "Like Newman in *Cool Hand Luke.* I was sure that deep down I was one of those guys. Too bad no one knew it but me, of course."

"So you dreamed you were James Dean and Paul Newman and—"

"No way," Pacey said, sipping his lemonade. "It's like you said. Dean died young, so he's frozen in his perfection. But Newman got old, and Brando got fa—"

Pacey stopped himself, heat coming to his face.

"Fat," Emily filled in. "You can say it, Pacey. It's not a dirty word."

She wiped her mouth with a yellow napkin. "Want to see my room?"

*God, no.*

"Sure."

He followed her upstairs and into a bedroom done in deep forest green. It was neat and orderly, with no high school memorabilia in view. Nothing. No pompoms, no awards, no clippings from the school paper, no honor roll certificates. Nothing.

It was like she had skipped the high school stage of life entirely.

Instead of the trappings of high school, a huge découpage mural hung on one wall. It was full of words, faces, bits of poetry, newspaper headlines.

He moved closer to study it.

"It's called 'Rant,' " Emily said.

72

Pacey's eyes flew over the images.

Faces of missing kids from the back of a milk carton. Dr. Kevorkian in the witness docket. Miss America. Gwyneth's head glued atop Camryn Mannheim's body and Camryn's glued atop Gwyneth's Oscar-night for-God's-sake-eat-a-hamburger! body. A photo from a protest of the Vietnam war. Bits of poetry by Langston Hughes and Allen Ginsberg. Monica Lewinsky's beret. Desmond Tutu. An anorexic girl and a supermodel, who weighed roughly the same, cut from magazines, with cartoon hands drawn so it appeared as if they had their arms around each other. A chubby little girl looking up at them.

"This thing is unbelievable," Pacey finally said.

"Thanks."

He turned to her. "You made it?"

She nodded.

"I didn't know you did art, Emily."

"And why should you know it? We're not really good friends."

"But what about school class—"

"I hate the art teacher," Emily said simply. "Judged me before she ever met me."

"I can relate to that." Pacey nodded, and looked back up at the huge mural. "So. Dare I ask you what your parents thought when they saw . . . this?"

"I don't know. Honestly, I don't."

Pacey raised his eyebrows. "You don't know?"

"Not what they thought. But I know what they did. They made me an instant appointment with the best shrink in Boston. I think they expected me to start dressing in black, pierce my tongue, and scar myself daily with a kitchen knife to let out the internal pain."

"What'd the shrink say?"

"She asked, 'how do *you* feel?' a lot. You know, your basic therapy wonk. Boring, banal, easy to fool."

Pacey laughed.

"Actually, I went to a therapist after that who was great. She loves 'Rant.' And she reassured my high-anxiety parents that I wasn't particularly crazy, just a deeply misunderstood, overly sensitive girl stuck in a small town where she never fit in before, doesn't fit in now, and never will fit in."

Pacey leaned against the wall. "That has a certain familiar ring to it. Although my father thinks shrinks are for sissies."

"Sissies?"

Pacey lowered his voice to a deep growl. "Not manly men like the manly men Witters."

"So, if you wanted to make him happy you should have dressed for the auction as, let's see—Jean-Claude Van Damme? Steven Seagal?"

"Maybe Jesse Ventura," Pacey replied. "Before he ran for office, of course. But any manly man who could kick the crap out of your basic Navy SEALS platoon with one hand tied behind his back would have done the trick."

"That's so *not* James Dean, huh?"

"Sheriff Witter considers James Dean amoral, illegal, and probably fatten—" Pacey stopped himself again.

He was such an *idiot.*

Emily ignored it. Or pretended to, he wasn't sure which.

She went over to her desk and took out a manila folder with some white paper in it.

"You'll never guess what this is," she said.

"True."

"It's a play I wrote," Emily said shyly. "Well, a part of a play."

She laughed self-consciously, and looked at Pacey. His face was impassive.

"A scene, anyway," she went on. She sat on her bed and glanced over at him again, like why didn't he join her on the bed, already?

He pretended not to get her unspoken signal and didn't budge.

"So, what's your scene about?"

"You can't laugh."

"Meaning you didn't write a comedy version of 'Rant,' " Pacey surmised.

"Actually, I wrote a scene for James Dean," Emily confessed. "I did this creative writing workshop at a writers' camp in June, and the professor said that a good writing exercise for beginning playwrights is to write a scene for someone you knew well."

"That kind of lets out a famous guy who died before you were born," Pacey said. "Wouldn't you agree?"

"Yeah," she agreed, fingering the pages in her hand. "But didn't you ever see a movie—I mean, a really great movie—and feel as if you knew a character in the movie better than you know someone in your own family?"

"Constantly," Pacey admitted.

75

She grinned at him. "I told you we have things in common. So anyway, let's read my scene."

"What do you mean? Like out loud?"

"Well, you can read it over first to yourself, I guess," Emily said. "Then we can work on it, and then we can act it out. That's the only way I'll really know if the scene works, you know? There are only two characters in it. James Dean and Natalie Wood. I changed the names, though, to protect the innocent."

She held the pages out to him.

*James Dean and Natalie Wood. Meaning I'm supposed to be Dean and Emily LaPaz is supposed to be—*

Pacey took the pages but still didn't join her on the bed. Quickly, he skimmed what Emily had written. The characters were named Peter and Esme, and they were boyfriend and girlfriend. The whole town was against them. But they had each other, blah-blah-blah. Then Pacey came to the final stage direction:

*Peter takes Esme into his arms and kisses her passionately.*

He closed his eyes and opened them again, hoping the directions would magically change to something like:

*Peter takes Esme's hand and shakes it warmly. Kisses her passionately.*

Still there. Damn.

"So, what do you think?" Emily asked. "Is it any good? On first reading, I mean."

"Interesting," Pacey said, as sweat popped out on his forehead. "But, hey, I'm no theater critic. You should probably work on this some more before we try to bring it to life, and I'm not a very good—"

"I've already worked on it a lot," Emily confessed. "Really, Pacey, with dialogue there's only so much you can do until you actually hear it and see it acted out. So I thought maybe we could bring it to life ourselves right now. Us two."

Pacey nodded earnestly, like one of those little annoying bobbing dogs in the back window of someone's car.

"Yep, yep, makes sense."

"So, you ready?"

Pacey grimaced. "Ooh."

"What's wrong?"

"Must have had too much lemonade. Where's the—?"

"Down the hall to the left, you'll see it."

"Thanks. Be right back." Pacey fled to the bathroom, shut the door behind him, and locked it.

He was stuck with Emily, alone in her house, about to do a scene where he had to kiss her passionately.

He eyed the window. It was a choice between a two-story drop to the ground or a passionate kiss with Emily LaPaz.

Suddenly he could not remember why he had ever wanted to raise money to save some stupid lighthouse.

\* \* \*

In front of Molly's Coffee Shop, Brett Ardor was on his knees polishing the black wingtips of Simon Fink, a sophomore computer dork. A carefully hand-lettered sign Joey had made hung around Brett's neck:

**Was I Ever Mean to You?**
**If So**
**Line Up for Free Shoeshine**

A long line of teens stood behind Simon.

"You missed a spot," Simon told Brett, pointing to his right shoe.

Brett swallowed the comeback that welled up and repolished Simon's right shoe.

"Decent," Simon pronounced, standing up to admire the shine. He looked over at Joey, who sat at one of the outdoor tables in front of the coffee shop. "Is tipping allowed?"

Joey mused a moment from her spot in the shade. "Only as it pertains to character improvement," she decided.

Simon nodded and turned back to Brett. " 'We all live in the prison of our own mind,' " he said.

"What, is that supposed to be deep or something?" Brett asked suspiciously.

"You'd have to ask Albert Einstein since he's the one who said it," Simon replied. "Thanks for the shine."

As Joey watched, a tall, gawky girl with bad skin sat in the chair and gave Brett a triumphant look. "Spit-shine, Ardor," she said. "And it had better be good. Or you'll be doing it again."

Brett began to shine her sandals. The truth was, Joey was amazed. So far Brett had done every single thing she'd ordered him to do. It wasn't like she could really make him wear that humiliating sign or shine all those shoes. He could get off his knees at any time, yell some Neanderthal insult in her direction, and take off.

But he didn't.

A girl Joey vaguely recognized from school, who worked part-time at the coffee shop, set a Coke on Joey's table.

"Wrong table," Joey said. "I didn't order this."

"Right table, it's on the house," the girl said. She looked over at Brett. "Watching Brett Ardor spit-shining shoes kinda brings tears to my eyes."

"It's for charity," Joey explained.

"Yeah, the lighthouse thing," the girl agreed. "But I still don't know how you got him to do it."

"Frankly, neither do I."

"You ought to make him do something really rank after this," the girl said, clearly relishing the thought. "Like maybe—I got it! Make him dress in drag and clean windshields with his butt!"

Joey grimaced. "That might be overkill."

"When it comes to Brett Ardor, no humiliation is overkill," the girl said. "Gotta go. Enjoy the Coke."

Joey took a thirsty slurp of the Coke and watched as the next person sat in front of Brett, proferring a sandaled foot.

"Mind if we join you?"

Joey looked up. It was Jen, still in her *Pleasantville* outfit. Jack was with her, dressed in normal Jack fashion.

"Brett Ardor humbly giving shoeshines to those he's wronged?" Jack exclaimed. "This is a surreal life moment."

"Pull up a smirk and join the club," Joey offered. "Or get in line for a shine, if you want."

"I'll pass," Jack said, as he and Jen sat down. "But how did you get him to do it?"

Joey shrugged. "He seems bizarrely willing to blindly follow orders."

"Gee, that makes Brett the son my father wishes he had," Jack joked.

Jen cocked her head at him. "I happen to think your father has a terrific son."

"I second that," Joey said. She eyed Brett, who wiped some sweat off his brow, then started on the girl's other shoe. "I'm having one of those life-changing realizations. Demeaning the deserving can be fun."

"I always knew you have more of the witchy woman in you than you wanted to cop to, Joey," Jen commented dryly.

*What, meaning I'm a bitch?* Joey thought. *Why am I always reading some hidden meaning into the things Jen says to me? Or is that exactly what she wants me to do?*

"So where's the guy who bid on you?" Joey asked her.

"Evidently that guy was a front for some other mystery guy who prefers to wrap himself in a shroud of anonymity," Jen explained. "I'm meeting said mystery guy in a little while. Frankly, I'm curious."

"Maybe it's Dawson," Joey said lightly, though there was an underlying edge to her voice.

Jen made a face. "First of all, why would he bother? And second of all, he's coming with me, to video the moment for posterity."

"Speaking of posterity, Joey," Jack began, "since Dawson isn't filming this epic moment, you ought to at least do some sketches of Brett in humble servitude mode. We could probably sell 'em for a mint."

"Highly doubtful," Joey said. "I'm not that good."

"Then why did *the* Mrs. Patricia Axworthy buy that sketch you did of Quinn in the lighthouse?" Jen asked.

Joey blushed. "She only did that because—"

"Someone bought one of your sketches, Joey?" Jack asked.

"Don't put a call in to the Louvre, okay?" Joey pushed her hair behind her ears self-consciously. "This very rich woman happened to see one of my sketches at the Bannermans' fund-raiser, and she bought it so it could be auctioned off for charity."

"But that's so great!" Jack reached for her hand. "Aren't you excited about it?"

"I'm sure she was just being nice. Or patronizing. Or both," Joey insisted.

"Trust me, a woman like that is never nice," Jen said. "The sketch was good. Who bought it?"

Joey shrugged.

"Wait, you're telling me you never checked to see who bought it or how much it sold for?" Jack asked.

"I was there waitressing, remember? And if those curried lamb thingies aren't served hot-hot-hot—"

Jack looked at Jen. "Do you know who bought it?"

*"If* anyone bought it," Joey corrected him.

"I'm done, I'm hot, I'm thirsty, I'm starving, and I gotta pee like a racehorse," Brett said, standing over her.

"Your manners overwhelm," Jen said.

Brett ignored her. "Joey?"

"You don't need permission to go into the coffee shop to use the men's room, Brett," Joey said.

"Duh. I kinda . . ." He hesitated, his eyes sliding over to Jen and Jack. He bent over and whispered into Joey's ear. "I kinda planned something for the girl who won me today. So I kinda thought we could go there."

"Where?" Joey asked, but Brett just looked uncomfortable.

Jen got up. "I have to go meet Dawson."

"And I just have to go," Jack said.

The two of them took off toward the school.

"Okay. Let's go," Brett said briskly.

"Let's review, Brett," Joey suggested. "I bid on you, not the other way around. That's why I'm the one who—"

"Yeah, yeah, can we just go?"

"Let me try that one word out on you again, Brett. Read my lips if it helps you keep up: 'Where'?"

Brett sighed. He fidgeted. And finally he spoke.

"Actually, it's a surprise. Please come."

Joey was completely taken aback. Brett sounded *normal.* Polite, even. He had actually said "please."

And she found herself replying, "All right."

# Chapter 8

"**Y**ou sure you don't mind helping me?" Dawson asked Jen, as they set up the video equipment outside the old movie theater downtown.

"It'll be fun," Jen replied. "And I don't have anything else to do until my one o'clock date with fate. Besides, watching Chris Wolfe humiliate himself is my sordid idea of a good time."

She'd gone back to Grams's house to talk with Jack, but he was in one of his I'd-rather-be-alone moods. Grams was with friends in the living room, discussing some church issue. So Jen had decided to go find Dawson again and see if she could give him a hand with the video until her mystery assignment.

She still liked being with Dawson more than she liked being with just about anyone else. Sometimes he seemed so innocent to her that she thought of him as a sweet, not-too-sophisticated, brother. Other times that very same lack of sophistication, combined with his passionate heart, made her wish she could go back to being a girl who could share that innocence. And then they could fall madly in love.

*Dream on, Jen*, she told herself. *You're over him. And as you keep telling yourself, a guy is not the answer to the problem, anyway. All a guy ever does is mask the loneliness for a while, he didn't really make it go away.*

*Hey, I'm one deep chick*, Jen thought sarcastically.

The street traffic was heavy, as tourists strolled in and out of the quaint shops, buying souvenirs or ice-cream cones, walking to the pier, enjoying the nice weather.

And heavy traffic was exactly what Heather Phillips wanted. She and Chris Wolfe, aka Elvis, were standing in front of the ice-cream parlor. She had set up speakers and a boombox as well as a microphone. Chris was reading over the lyrics she'd written.

Lyrics that, she had informed him, "Elvis" was about to sing.

"Ready?" Heather called to Dawson. "I want every moment of this saved for posterity."

"Just about," Dawson called back.

Chris looked up from the lyric sheet she'd given him. "Man, I don't want to do this—"

"That's exactly the point, Elvis," Heather said sweetly. "But you're mine for the afternoon, big boy, so go get 'em." She stepped up to the microphone, tapped it once to make sure it was on. "Ladies and gentlemen," her amplified voice called out, "as a special Capeside attraction, our very own Elvis impersonator, Chris Wolfe, will do his very *personal* rendition of 'Hound Dog.' "

Dawson began filming as curious tourists stopped to watch. Heather applauded and knelt down to press the on button on her tape deck. The instrumental opening of "Hound Dog" filled the air. Heather gestured to Chris to step up to the mike.

He cleared his throat nervously and began to sing the lyrics Heather had given him.

"I ain't nothin' but a Hound Dog
I use girls all the time.
I ain't nothin' but a Hound Dog
I give 'em all a line.
I ain't nothin' but a user and my face matches
my behind.

"You say I got no class
I'm nothin' but a slime.
You say I got no class
Should stick with my own kind.
'Cuz I ain't nothin' but a user and my face
matches my behind.
Yeah I'm nothin' but a user and my face matches
my behind."

The instrumental soundtrack came to a rousing rock 'n' roll finish. People applauded, laughing and pointing at Chris. The little kids thought it was so funny, some of them actually fell on the sidewalk laughing. One kid turned around and stuck his butt out, shaking it at Chris, singing, "This is your be-hind!" His friends joined in, a kid chorus singing the last line, shaking their booties at Chris.

"You know, Dawson, few moments in life are quite as perfect as this one," Jen said happily, as she watched Chris squirm. "Heather Phillips is my new idol."

Joey and Brett strolled over to the ice-cream store just as Chris was finishing his performance. The crowd blocked Joey's view of Dawson, or else she would have headed in the other direction immedi-ately. Instead, she told Brett to purchase her a triple-dip chocolate-chip cone with sprinkles, while she lolled in the sun.

*It's really so much more fun to be served than to be the one serving,* Joey decided. *And it's going to be a real joy to tell Brett Ardor what to do all day long.*

"So, Brett, I've been thinking of just what I'd like you to do for me today," Joey said, as she licked her ice-cream cone.

"I'm supposed to be Mark McGwire," he re-minded her.

"Right," Joey agreed. "Who swings such a big stick. . . . Glad you trashed that sign, by the by."

"Only because you made me."

"That's true, I did." She took another bite of ice cream. "So, Brett—oh, I'm sorry, *Mark.* Here's the first thing you're going to do when we finish eating this ice cream. You're going to—"

"Hold it, hold it," Brett said. "I got a whaddaya-call-it—a counteroffer."

Joey raised her eyebrows, waiting.

"Okay, so you bought me for fifty-one cents, right?"

"Kind of humiliating, huh?" Joey sympathized.

"Damn straight," Brett agreed.

"Frankly, I was hoping I wouldn't have to bid over a quarter," Joey said with a shrug.

Brett scowled. "Ha-ha, very funny. Here's my counteroffer. I'll pay you five bucks to drop this whole thing."

"Five bucks, huh?"

Brett nodded. "See, you end up ahead financially, is what happens. I figure you could use the bucks. And I could get out of this."

"It's so thoughtful of you to consider my finances," Joey oozed. "The answer is, forget it."

"Six bucks."

Joey shook her head.

Brett turned his palms up. "Ten, okay? And that's my final offer. Ten whole dollars must mean a lot to a chick like you."

Joey fixed her eyes on him. "I'm curious, Brett. Just exactly what is 'a chick like me'?"

He shrugged. "You know. Poor. Weird. Weird sister. Your dad's this total lowlife, right? You're decent looking, you know. I mean I got a load of those nudie shots of you on the Internet and you gotta admit you've got a great set of—"

"Brett? Excuse me for interrupting what I'm sure was going to be a fascinating discourse on my life, my finances, and my anatomy," Joey said. "First of all, I was not nude in those shots on the Internet. That is just your sleazy little imagination at work.

And I do emphasize the word *little*. As in microscopic. Which matches the size of your sensitivity, your brain, and most probably your anatomical endowment, though that last part is just a guess on my part."

"My *what*?" Brett sputtered.

"Compensating for your shortcomings with that pathetic 'big bat' sign and all," Joey went on. "But forgive me, your life is pathetic enough without my throwing it in your face. So let's get back to your financial offer. Ten bucks to buy your freedom. Tempting. For a 'chick' like me. But no sale."

"Oh, come on, gimme a major break—"

"Stand up, Brett," Joey instructed, polishing off her ice-cream cone. "Now, every time I see anyone you've ever insulted, you are going to go up to that person, get down on one knee, take that person's hand, and sincerely apologize for what you said or did."

At that moment, a break in the crowd allowed Joey a clear view of Jen and Dawson. Chris was now doing a Heather-written version of "Blue Suede Shoes."

"Didn't you once make some horrible remark to Heather about the size of her breasts?"

"What breasts?"

"Exactly," Joey said. "So as soon as Chris is done humiliating himself, you are to go over to Heather, get down on one knee, and apologize."

"What, like, 'I'm sorry I once asked you if you glued two gumdrops to a sheet of typing paper and stuck it under your T-shirt'?" He smirked.

"Repeating the insult isn't exactly what I had in

mind." She handed him a sheet of paper. "I've written it out for you. Read it word for word. Or do
you need help reading it?"

"Ha-ha, big joke."

Chris finished singing. Joey cocked her head at
Brett, indicating he should head for Heather.

Brett cursed under his breath and lumbered
across the street to Heather, who was picking up
her boombox. He dropped to one knee in front of
her.

"Hey, look, that guy's proposing to that girl!" a
little girl cried, tugging on her mother's hand.

"Isn't that sweet, honey?" her mom said. "Let's
watch!"

Brett took a startled Heather's hand. "Believe me,
Phillips, this isn't my idea." She tried to pull away
but he held on tight, reading off Joey's paper.

"I would like to tell you, fill-in-the-person's-
name-here," Brett read, "that in the past I have been
a mean, insensitive idiot, clod, cretin, jerk, fool, and
all-around pathetic excuse for a human being. And
I would like to apologize to you, fill-in-the-person's-
name-here. I will try to become a better person."

Dawson panned his camera from Joey, in front of
the ice-cream parlor, to the sidewalk, where Brett
was reading the apology script to Heather.

"Priceless," Jen murmured.

"How interesting," Heather replied. "How touching. And how delightful to have two such odious
human specimens groveling at my feet."

Brett got up, giving Heather the evil eye. "Happy
now, Phillips?"

"Kinda," Heather decided. "Tell Joey I said

thanks. Oh, and just a tip, Brett. Where it says fill-in-the-person's-name-here, that's where you're supposed to fill in the person's name."

Brett snorted. "Like I care."

He sighed a long-suffering sigh and headed back for Joey.

Heather turned to Chris. "We're havin' some fun now, huh? And just wait until you hear what I've got planned for you next, Elvis, honey." She looked around for Dawson, because she wanted to make sure he captured the next stage of the Chris Wolfe humiliation. But he had followed Brett back to the chairs outside the ice-cream parlor.

"Okay, Brett, we're moving on," Joey said, getting up quickly.

"I thought you wanted to stay here so that I could—"

Joey refused to look at Dawson, even though his camera was aimed at her. "I changed my mind."

"Why did you bid on Brett, Joey?" Dawson asked from behind his lens.

"I don't want to be in the video, Dawson," Joey said, her voice low. She wouldn't make eye contact with him.

"Come on, Joey, it's for charity," Jen reminded her. "Everyone's gonna be in it."

"Except me," Joey snapped.

Brett smiled into the camera, stuck his tongue out and waggled it. "Gonna make me a star, dude?"

"Sorry, belching on cue won't get you *The Real World*," Jen told him. "They covered that one a few seasons back."

"We're leaving, Brett," Joey insisted.

"Good doggie," Jen said, reaching up to pat him on the head. "Go, boy."

"Wait, I think I insulted Lindley a whole buncha times," Brett jeered. "You know. Like how she's doin' the bootie thang with, like, everyone in the entire—"

"Besides being unbelievably rude and insulting," Dawson interrupted, "that also happens to be a lie."

"Why, 'cuz you never did her?" Brett smirked.

"Just out of curiosity," Dawson asked, "does it ever bother you to be as imbecilic as you are?"

"Brett!" Joey called angrily. "We're leaving."

Brett got in Dawson's face. "I'm on to you, artsy-boy. You probably made a video of you and that swisher Jack—"

"Knees! Now!" Joey had marched back over to him and was screaming in his face.

"Man, this is all bull—"

Dawson grabbed Brett's T-shirt. "She *owns* you, Brett. So I suggest you do what she says. Or I will make you do it."

"You and what army?" Brett scoffed.

Jen and Heather moved in. "This army," Jen said sweetly.

Brett groaned and got down on his knees.

"Apologize to Jen. Then apologize to Dawson," Joey instructed him.

"I don't want his apology, actually," Dawson said.

Jen shrugged. "Neither do I."

Joey nodded. "New orders, Brett. Read your prepared apology. Over and over and over. Loud. Because I'm sure at one time or another you've been mean, nasty, and deliberately cruel under a pathetic

91

guise of humor to just about everyone. So we'll go for the cover apology."

"Use my sound system," Heather offered. "Chris and I are moving on to Phase Two, and we won't be needing it."

"What the hell is Phase Two?" Chris asked.

Heather grinned.

Brett went over to the microphone. Jen lowered it and he got down on his knees.

"You're on, Brett," Jen said. "Into the mike."

"I would like to tell you, fill-in-the-person's-name-here, that in the past I have been a mean, insensitive . . ."

Dawson was getting it all on film. "This is great, Joey. Poetic justice purchased for the princely sum of—"

He looked over his shoulder.

Joey was gone.

*Chapter 9*

Jen and Dawson stood under the flagpole in front of the school. Dawson looked at his watch. "It looks like your mystery guy stood you up."

"I might bother to take it personally if I knew who the hell he was," Jen said, leaning against the pole.

Dawson aimed his video camera at her. "So, Jen, you chose to dress like Reese Witherspoon's character in *Pleasantville*. Is it because you relate to what she went through in the film?"

Jen glared at the camera lens. "Imagine. So young and yet so perceptive."

Dawson ignored her sarcasm. "So, do you think that the mystery guy who bid for your company today was bidding on you, Jen, or on the character from the movie?"

Jen was getting irritated. "Gee, Dawson, I don't know. If he ever shows up, we can ask him."

*Maybe Dawson is your mystery guy,* Joey had said.

No, couldn't be. And yet here she was, at the flag-pole. And the only guy in sight was Dawson. And wasn't he just romantic enough to—

*Dawson.*

*But I'm over him. I am.*

And yet gazing at him now, with the sun glinting off his hair as he filmed her, the old feelings came flooding back. How she had felt in his arms. How his tender kisses had turned hot, then hotter still. But the passion had come from caring, not just from lust or hormones or loneliness. Because he cared about her, really truly cared.

*Dawson.*

Jen cocked her head at him. "Dawson, put the camera down."

He kept filming her. "Sorry, Jen, but this time you're the subject, which means you don't call the shots. So, do you have any feelings about a guy who would bid for your company, hide behind someone else, and then not even bother to show up?"

Jen grinned. "I do."

"And those feelings would be—?"

Pushing his camera down, she moved close to him and ran one hand through his hair. "You are one of a kind, Dawson Leery."

He had that endearingly Dawson bewildered look on his face. "Thank you," he said. "I think."

Jen laughed. "You're good, I'll give you that. As long as Dawson Leery lives and breathes, true romance will never die because—"

"Jen Lindley?"

Jen turned around. A very hot guy she'd never seen before—different from the guy who'd bid on her at the auction—stood before her.

Sun-streaked blond hair. Patrick Swayze circa *Dirty Dancing* body. Eyes hidden behind dark sunglasses. He had a motorcycle helmet under his arm; his top-of-the-line Harley was parked at the curb. Jen had been so involved talking with Dawson that she hadn't even heard him arrive.

"That's me," she said.

The guy looked from Jen, to Dawson, and back to Jen. "You're waiting for your mystery date, correct?"

Jen looked at Dawson. "I thought I had already found him," she murmured sadly.

Dawson was so busy filming that Jen's comment didn't really register. This was going to make a great sequence in his video.

"So, you chose to keep your identity a secret up until now," Dawson said, his camera aimed at the guy. "Why? And who are you?"

"That's not important," the guy said.

Emotions flitted through Jen like a film on fast forward: confusion, disappointment, embarrassment, hurt.

And anger.

At herself. For being such a vulnerable wuss, still.

*Never let 'em see you sweat, Jennifer,* her dad used to tell her. *They see you sweat, it's all over.*

Time to go into as-if mode.

"I'd say it's fairly important," Jen said, swallowing her hurt and flashing the mystery guy a coquettish smile. "I mean, you did go to a lot of trouble. I have to admit that I'm flattered. I also have to admit that although you obviously know who I am, I don't know who you are."

He handed her an envelope.

"What's this?"

"Your mystery date wishes for you to read this letter after I leave," the cute guy explained.

Jen stared at the envelope. "Wait, wait. You're telling me that you're not him, either?"

"Correct. Have a nice day." The guy turned and walked toward his Harley.

"But this is crazy!" Jen called to him. "Who gave you this letter for me? Hey, I'm talking to you!"

The guy didn't answer. He got on his Harley and revved off.

Jen angrily tore open the envelope and read the typed letter aloud.

My dear Ms. Lindley,

Thank you for following the instructions thus far. Please be at Dunn's Lighthouse at three o'clock this afternoon. Come alone. This is the last time you will hear from me through a third party.

"There's something very bizarre about this, Jen," Dawson said. "I don't like it."

"I'm not exactly turning cartwheels, either." She stuck the letter in her pocket and turned away from Dawson.

*How could I have ever thought it was him? Stupid, stupid—*

"Jen?"

"Don't say it, Dawson."

"My mind seems to be lagging a few beats behind in the realization department," he said. "Or else I'm having an incredibly narcissistic moment. Did you . . . did you think I was your mystery guy?"

She turned to him. "Why, is it so difficult to believe that you might want to bid for my company?"

"No, not at all. It's just that . . . why would I go about it in such a strange way?"

"I wasn't thinking 'strange,' " Jen confessed. "I was thinking 'romantic.' And please do not add to my current humiliation by protesting that you would have bid on me if you had thought of it, or by doing that Dawson thing you do where you attempt to define in painful detail just exactly what your feelings for me are at this point, or—"

"There's no reason for you to feel anything negative about this in any way, Jen," Dawson assured her. "And the only thing I feel is flattered."

"Hey, if a true friend can't boost your ego, who can?"

Dawson nodded. "I seem to be much better at true friendship than I am at true love these days."

A smile curled Jen's lip. "When I was about eight, I went to see *Edward Scissorhands,* and I fell madly in love with Johnny Depp as Edward. There was this boy in my class who was an albino—although at the time I had no idea what that was—but he had white hair and eyelashes and he was kind of quiet and strange, so I was sure he was deep and sensitive, just like Edward. I wrote him love notes that he never acknowledged, but I thought he was just shy, like Edward. So finally, I asked my mother, 'How do you know if a guy really loves you?' "

"What did she say?" Dawson asked.

"She said, 'He really loves you if you're his wife and he spends more money on your birthday present than he does on his girlfriend's.' "

For a moment, Dawson was silent. "I'm sorry, Jen."

She shrugged. "Regret strikes me as a quaint but rather ridiculous notion, Dawson. There are countless things about my mother I dislike intensely, but her brutal honesty isn't one of them."

"More like bitter cynicism," Dawson said. "I never had to ask my parents about love because I saw it demonstrated every day. And I'm so sorry you didn't have that, Jen."

Jen gave a bitter laugh. "Where's your appreciation of irony, Dawson? Your oh-so-in-love parents who are still oh-so-in-love have split up, remember? While my can't-stand-each-other-and-never-could-stand-each-other parents are still together."

"My parents are only temporarily estranged," Dawson insisted. "Even the greatest love can—does—hit walls that seem insurmountable at times, but you can't give up. Ever."

*He means Joey*, Jen thought. *Him and Joey. Forever.*

The realization made her ache. Not so much because she wanted Dawson but because she wanted that kind of love.

And she was afraid she'd never, ever find it.

"Love is an illusion, Dawson," Jen said. "Just another thing we invented to make us feel better, or not give up hope, or numb the pain. Like drugs. Or alcohol. Or sex. Or religion. Whatever gets you through the—"

Jen suddenly realized that Dawson was no longer looking at her, but *past* her. She turned around to see what he was looking at.

Joey. Walking by with Brett Ardor. Of course, Joey.

*We are such a cliché*, Jen thought. She had to laugh. *If my life was a movie, I'd demand a refund.*

"Joey and Brett." Jen frowned, feigning deep concern. "I'd be deeply worried if I were you, Dawson."

Joey. God, just seeing her apart from him made him feel . . .

*Things I don't want to feel right now*, Dawson thought. *And I definitely do not want to talk about Joey with Jen right now. Which calls for a neat change of subject.*

He tore his eyes away from Joey, who was laughing at something Brett was saying. "You're not actually planning to go meet this guy at the lighthouse later, are you?"

"Sure," Jen said. "Why not?"

"Teen girl agrees to meet strange guy at remote lighthouse? It's highly reminiscent of a bad teen horror flick, Jen."

"Quinn is there, remember?" Jen reminded him.

"Somehow the additional presence of Quinn Bickfee doesn't fill me with reassurance of your safety. So if you're going, I'm coming with you."

"I'm on to you, Dawson."

He looked bewildered. "What?"

"While you may have some concern for my safety, you have a lot more concern for your video. In other words, you want the footage."

"Well, yes, but that's not the reason that I—"

"Analytical meltdown has just commenced. Let's go film some fake celebs." She pulled him away from the flagpole. "We'll pretend we're just a couple of small-town all-American teens with nothing deeper or darker on our minds than filming other small-town all-American teens taking part in a celeb look-alike auction for charity. I've always been a sucker for a fairy tale."

"This way," Brett told Joey, as they cut across a rarely used trail in the park.

Irritation crept up the back of Joey's neck. At herself, not Brett. She had actually agreed to get in his car and go with him to—well, she still didn't know to where. Somewhere in the park, evidently.

"Listen, Brett, change of plans," Joey announced. "We're heading back to your car as of now. Then we're—"

"It's not much farther." He cut through some thorny bushes and held the branches back so she could get by, then led her to an even more remote dirt path.

"Uh, Earth to Brett!" Joey called. "Ground control to Mark McGwire? We are leaving! As of—"

"We're here," Brett said.

Joey could see that. What she couldn't do was speak because she was too amazed.

Under a leafy oak tree was a blanket. On which was a pristine white linen tablecloth. On which was a picnic basket, a cooler, two crystal goblets, and place settings for two.

And in the center of it all was a small vase holding wildflowers.

"You did this?" Joey managed.

"No, I hired that caterer jerk, Gullet," Brett snorted sarcastically. "He's in the cooler. Cooling."

Joey laughed.

"So, you're here. You might as well sit down," Brett said.

She did.

So did he. He opened the cooler and took out a sweating bottle of sparkling cider, popped it open, and poured some into both goblets. Then he clinked his glass against hers. "So, here's to—to what?"

"To saving the lighthouse," Joey said.

"Yeah." They both took long drinks. Brett took food out of the picnic basket and cooler—cheese, pâté, French bread, strawberries, grapes. The feast just kept coming.

Joey just shook her head. "I have to say, I'm amazed."

Brett just shrugged and dug deeper into the picnic basket, bringing out more food. Chips, nuts, crackers, caramel corn. And a box wrapped in silver paper, tied with a blue ribbon.

"This is for you." He thrust the box at her.

Joey opened it. It was a box of imported, hand-dipped, heart-shaped chocolate truffles, each in its own silver or gold foil wrapper.

"When I was a kid I used to go into that specialty food store that used to be downtown, remember?" Joey asked, gazing at the chocolates. "It closed a long time ago. I used to love to go in there and look at the fancy food. And I'd see the boxes of really expensive chocolates, like this one, and they looked so . . . I don't know . . . magical or something. And I always wished I could have one."

"So, now you do. Chocolate gives me zits, so you don't need to share," Brett said.

Joey unwrapped a truffle and took a bite. She closed her eyes as the chocolate melted in her mouth. "I was right. It tastes magical."

"Know what's great about not bein' a little kid anymore?" Brett asked. "You get to eat dessert first."

"You're right," Joey agreed, as she popped another truffle into her mouth. Brett broke off a huge hunk of French bread and some cheese and began to chow down.

After four truffles, Joey took another sip of her sparkling cider. "So, you did all of this without knowing what girl was going to bid on you?"

Brett popped a grape into his mouth. "I figured any girl who bid on me would have to like me. So this could be a happenin' little thing."

Now it all made sense. Joey put down the box of chocolates. "In other words, this private little dining experience was supposed to be *Prelude to a Kiss*?"

"Huh?" Utter confusion on the part of Brett.

"Lunch before the booty call out here in nature?"

"You mean did I think I was gonna get some? Get real."

" 'Real' is not what I'm getting at the moment, Brett," Joey snapped. She jumped up and grabbed her backpack. "Try furious, disgusted, livid, pissed-off beyond—"

"I was afraid no one would bid on me, okay?" Brett yelled.

Joey just stood there.

"I thought I'd just be standing up there and no one would give two cents for me," Brett went on. "I never woulda been one of the celebrities in the first place except my buddies bet me I was too chicken to do it. So then I had to, you know? And I thought—if some girl actually bids money to spend the day with me so that I'm not humiliated in front of everyone in the entire town, I'm gonna treat that girl right. End of story."

Joey sat down again.

"We can leave this stuff and go back and I'll do whatever stupid stuff you want me to do," Brett said. His voice was low now. "Just don't tell anyone what I just told you, okay?"

Silence. Joey watched an ant make away with a bread crumb. "Okay," she finally said.

Brett got busy making bread balls, flicking the pellets at the tree. Anything so he wouldn't have to look at her, Joey figured. She hugged her knees to her chin and circled her arms around them. "I draw. Kind of. I mean, I *try* to draw."

Brett scratched his head. "Did I miss something?"

"I'm what you could call financially challenged at the moment," Joey went on, not answering his question. "So I was waitressing at the Bannerman fund-raiser. This rich woman there saw a sketch I did of Quinn in the lighthouse, and she put it in the blind auction. And I was so afraid that no one would bid on my drawing that I never even checked to see if it sold."

Her eyes met his, and she forced herself to keep talking. "And I thought, if someone actually did bid on it, I would feel so grateful to that person."

She saw the light dawn in his eyes, then he shrugged self-consciously. "I bet someone bought it. And for a lot more than fifty-one cents, too."

Suddenly, Brett got very busy eating again so he wouldn't have to look at her.

For once, Joey was beyond words. Shame was what she felt. But the feeling was so much bigger than that one, measly little syllable that uttering it would only add insult to injury.

"Brett, can I ask you a question?"

"Go ahead."

"Why are you mean? Why do you make fun of people?"

"I'm just fooling around. People take everything so *serious* all the time. They need to lighten up."

"But if you see that you're hurting their feelings—"

"Dummy," Brett barked.

Joey was taken aback. "Pardon me?"

"That's my old man's pet name for me," he filled in. "Also ree-tard. And jerk-off."

"That's horrible," Joey said.

Brett shrugged. "What's the biggie? It's just words."

"Words can hurt a lot," Joey insisted.

"Lotsa things hurt, if you let 'em," Brett said. "He never used me or my ma for a punching bag, like my friend's old man used to do. He works two jobs to pay the bills. And he comes to every single one of my football games. He's there for me. So what's a few names? I figure. Nothin'."

Joey stared into the distance, seeing nothing. *My father loves me and calls me sweetheart,* she thought. *But he lied to me. Betrayed me. Broke my heart.*

"My father would never call me names, but when I needed him, he wasn't there," Joey confessed over the lump in her throat. "And he never will be again."

"Everyone has their story," Brett said, philosophically. "That's the way it is."

"That's the way it is," Joey echoed. She picked up the box of chocolates and held them out to him. "Truffle?"

"I love chocolate," Brett groaned, "but I swear the stuff gives me zits the size of a friggin' grape and then no way can I get a date for the—"

"Yo, Brett," Joey interrupted. "I own you, remember? Meaning that for the moment, I am your date. By choice. So eat a truffle."

He ate two.

# Chapter 10

"**T**he best," Emily declared, as the final credits for *Rebel Without a Cause* rolled across the big-screen TV in her parents' family room. She got up from the couch and pulled a string on the venetian blinds, allowing the afternoon sun to pour into the room.

"Classic," Pacey agreed from the BarcaLounger.

"Jim Stark is just so sensitive. I fall in love with him again every time I see the movie," Emily admitted.

"You know, I could watch it over and over and still find new things in it, couldn't you?" Pacey asked brightly. "In fact, maybe we should watch it again now just to really inspire your writing—"

"I'm inspired now," Emily assured him. She pushed the buttons on the BarcaLounger remote control to rewind the videotape, and she sat on the armrest by Pacey, smiling down at him. "I have to thank you. It was a great idea you came up with, our watching *Rebel* together before we do my scene."

Pacey smiled back and did that stupid nodding thing with his head again.

*I am having a Jim Stark moment*, Pacey thought. *Nowhere to run, nowhere to hide.*

Emily glanced at her watch. "Wow, it's past four o'clock already. I can't believe it."

*Me neither*, Pacey thought glumly. *The celebrity auction day ends at six. And there is no way I can get out of doing that scene for another two hours.*

He'd stalled. And he'd stalled. But he couldn't stall any longer. James Dean and Natalie Wood, also known as Pacey Witter and Emily LaPaz, were about to head up to Emily's bedroom. To share a passionate kiss.

"Let's just clean up in here a little," Emily said, as she gracefully started to gather up empty junk-food packages and soda cans. "Then we can go back upstairs and get to work."

"Sounds like a plan," Pacey said, with as much enthusiasm as he could muster.

*It's not that Emily isn't a perfectly nice person*, Pacey thought, as he helped her gather up the trash. *It's just that she's so . . . her butt is so—*

"Huge," Emily said, nodding with satisfaction.

"Wh-what?" Pacey stammered, red-faced. Had he lost his mind and said it out loud or something?

"Huge improvement," Emily explained. "You know. In living room tidiness. My mother is only happy when she lives in a place where there are no signs that anyone is actually alive there."

"Really," Pacey remarked, as if this were a fascinating bit of information. He sat back in the Barca-Lounger. "Tell me more about her."

"Honestly, I'd rather not. You ready?"

"Sure." Pacey got up and trudged up the stairs behind Emily. Behind Emily's behind.

*You suck, Witter,* he told himself. *She's nice. She's smart. Try being gracious and just doing the scene and kiss her once and—*

"You know I have a girlfriend, right?" Pacey blurted out when they reached her bedroom.

"Andie McPhee," Emily said, reaching for the pages of her scene on her desk. "I like her."

"Me, too," Pacey agreed. "More than."

"That's nice." She smiled at him, handing him his copy of her scene. "I've got a copy, too."

"Wonderful." Pacey scanned it, as he walked to the doorway, putting as much distance as he could between Emily and himself.

"What are you going over there for?"

"To . . . enter," Pacey invented. "You know. Make an entrance."

"But the scene starts with Natalie and James already together and already in love," Emily pointed out.

"Uh, Peter and Esme," Pacey said. "That's what you call them here. Interesting name, Esme. How did you happen to think of it?" Pacey lolled against the wall, excruciatingly casual.

Emily shrugged. "I just like it. Anyway, they're in the middle of an emotional crisis. I really think they'd be close to each other. Physically."

"Physically," Pacey echoed.

Emily nodded. "Right, right, that would make sense."

Pacey didn't move.

"But you know, now that I think about it, it's an interesting choice to start with space between them," Emily mused thoughtfully. "Our professor at writing camp called it playing the opposites—you know, like how distance can add to intimacy."

"Absolutely!" Pacey agreed. "See, that's what I was saying. Thinking. It's *so* much more intimate if I'm way over here."

Emily looked down at her script. Pacey waited. And waited. And waited. Maybe she was getting into character or something. Hopefully, it would take her a really long time.

"Pacey? You have the first line," Emily pointed out.

"Right!"

*Go for bad acting*, he decided. *As in total lack of emotion. Good tack.*

"My parents just don't understand, Esme," Pacey read, with all the feeling he'd put into reading aloud the ingredients off the cereal box while he chewed his Cheerios. "I can't take it anymore. All I want to do—"

"Is to dress how you want and be who you are," Emily read as Esme, her voice full of emotion.

"But it's no use," Pacey/Peter read, his voice still a monotone. "They're beating me down."

"You're stronger than they are!" declared Emily/Esme.

"No," from Pacey/Peter.

"Yes! And with my love for you, we can be stronger together than they will ever be!"

"Esme," Pacey/Peter intoned, "do you know how much your love means to me? Without it, I'm nothing. But if you—"

"Cut, cut," Emily called, tossing her script on her bed. "Damn. It sucks."

"No, it doesn't," Pacey insisted, and now his voice had all the emotion it had lacked during the scene. "Really, it's good."

"Please, it's so trite." She sat on the edge of her bed, thoroughly dejected. "I really thought it might be good. But it's not."

Guilt washed over him. He had wrecked her scene, and he knew it. And he'd done it just so he wouldn't have to kiss her.

"Emily, I am so, so sorry," Pacey said.

And he was. Sorry for what he'd done. Sorry for her.

He went and sat next to her on the bed. "Listen, Emily," he began gently, "I was thinking that—"

"Wait, I know what I did wrong." She jumped up and strode over to her computer, booted it up, and wordlessly clicked her mouse until she came to the word-processing document that held the Esme/Peter scene.

Pacey wandered over, not knowing what else to do, to look over her shoulder.

"It's not your fault, Pacey," Emily told him sincerely. "It wasn't what you were doing. It's clearly a problem in the writing."

"But—"

"A problem that can be fixed." She scrolled down to the beginning of the scene.

"But—"

"Pacey, no offense but shut up," Emily said. "Go read a book or watch a video with the sound off or something."

"Emily, to be perfectly honest, I don't think the problem was—"

Emily spun around in her chair. "Don't you remember how I told you that sometimes you can't get the spine of a scene until you actually hear it aloud?" She waited expectantly.

"Yeah," Pacey said, finally.

"Well, I heard enough to know that I was on the wrong track. And there's no time like the present to do the rewrites. So can I please get to work?"

"Yes ma'am." Pacey backed away from her. Fine. Whatever. He had tried, hadn't he? "I'm just going to take a look at 'Rant' one more time, and then you'll find me . . . uh . . . reading a magazine."

But Emily was already at work at her computer, adding lines, deleting lines, and even mouthing them quietly to herself. Pacey had seen Dawson do the same thing many times and knew that when Dawson was writing, it was like he was in a world of his own.

Now Emily was in that world. And it didn't matter that her celebrity date with Pacey Witter as James Dean was slipping through the hourglass.

Pacey wandered back over to "Rant." There was a light switch on the wall near it, and he flipped it on, which caused the track lighting to illuminate Emily's work even more clearly.

*Amazing*, Pacey thought. *Really awesome.*

The whole thing was protected by a thin, clear acrylic sheet that was anchored to the wall by a series of clamps. Emily had explained to him earlier that it allowed her to take the acrylic off and add to her work whenever she wanted to. A work in progress stretching into the infinite, she had called it.

"Hey, Em—" Pacey started to ask her how often she worked on "Rant," but realized that Emily was still intent on her rewrites, and cut himself off. He looked again at the piece. The longer he looked at it, the less haphazard it appeared. In fact, it seemed to be, in some way, brilliantly organized. It seemed to be divided into loose segments—one part dealing with society, one part dealing with art and music, one part with sports, one part with body image, and so forth.

"Pacey?"

Pacey jumped. He'd been so absorbed in her mural he hadn't even heard her walk over to him.

"Huh?"

Emily smiled. "I've been finished writing for ten minutes," she said softly. "But I didn't want to disturb you. You were so . . . concentrated."

"Sorry," Pacey said. "I didn't realize you'd finished. I just got so into this." He turned back to "Rant." "It's like—like it says *everything*."

"It does." She touched one finger to the clear acrylic covering. "But on the other hand, everything changes, doesn't it?"

"Yeah, it does," Pacey whispered, his eyes searching over the "Rant" images. But instead of seeing

"Rant," he saw Pacey the loser. Pacey and Andie. Pacey the changed man. Pacey without Andie. Scared, lonely Pacey.

Suddenly, he missed Andie so much, it was like a fist in his gut.

*What am I doing here? Why don't I go to Providence and grab her and bring her back here where she belongs, because without her I'm—*

"Pacey?" Emily asked hesitantly. "Are you okay?"

He didn't speak, just smiled sadly. Funny. Andie thought he was her knight in shining armor.

When all along it had been her, saving him.

# Chapter 11

"**P**acey? We don't have to do the new lines if you don't want to," Emily said softly.

Pacey blinked. Rubbed his hand over his face. Flew back from the there and then to the here and now. "No, it's okay. Let's do it."

She regarded him thoughtfully, then finally handed him the new pages. "I think the problem was that Esme was just too flat," Emily explained. "So let's try it this way."

Pacey was tempted to look at the last page, to see if the Esme/Peter kiss was still in it, but he knew that would be unbelievably bad form.

*I'll just have to wing it,* he thought. *And if the kiss is there, the kiss is—*

"Pacey?"

"Uh, right, here goes." Pacey cleared his throat,

and when he began again, he really did try to put some meaning into the lines Emily had written.

"I can't take it anymore," Pacey/Peter read. "I'm a chicken. My dad's right. But I look at you, Esme, and I see a girl who's never afraid."

"But I'm afraid all the time." Emily/Esme stepped closer to Pacey.

"Are you kidding?" Pacey/Peter asked. "But you seem so strong all the time. When those preppy, cool kids are mean to you, it never gets to you."

"It gets to me," Emily/Esme said. "It gets to me just like it gets to you, Peter. And if I hide it better, it's only because I'm even more afraid of letting them see how much they hurt me than you are. Everyone suffers, Peter."

She moved closer to him, and Pacey was surprised to realize he had unconsciously moved closer to her as well. They stood in the middle of Emily's room, mere inches from each other.

Pacey looked down at his script, then he looked into Emily's eyes and read his line. "Everyone?"

For a moment, they stared into each other's eyes. And her eyes were beautiful, Pacey realized. Not just nice, but really beautiful.

Emily turned abruptly and went to sit at her computer.

"Well?" she asked.

He looked down at the script again. "That's not the next line," Pacey pointed out. "The next line is Peter's, and he says, 'Esme, for God's—' "

"I know the line, I wrote it." She smiled at him. "I wanted to know, was the scene any more honest?"

Pacey gazed at her. Edges blurred. And he saw

not the Emily his age with the almost-pretty face and the distorted proportions that hid her true, amazing self from everyone, unwilling to risk them laughing at her any more than they already laughed at her.

Instead, he saw her as the little girl she must have been before she'd learned to be so afraid.

And then, another magical bizarre time warp, as he saw himself there, in Emily's chair, as a little boy. Seven or eight, maybe. Face anxious. Making a joke to cover it up. Always in big brother Doug's shadow. Trying his best, but knowing that his best would never be good enough.

*Everyone suffers.*

"Okay, I'm assuming your elongated silence means you hated my rewrites," Emily said, sighing. "Too melodramatic, huh?"

Back to Earth. To now.

"Emily, it was lovely."

Her face softened, grew hopeful. "It was?"

"It was."

"You don't have to say that just because I paid money to spend the afternoon with James Dean, you know," she said, dimples appearing as she grinned.

"I assure you, I am being completely honest." He sat on her bed, staring across the room at "Rant."

*Everyone suffers*, he heard her say again in his head.

And he thought of all the times that he'd heard people cracking on her outsized butt, or about how no guy would go out with her on a bet, or about how if she went swimming she was a walking tidal—

He flushed red for an instant. Because he knew that he'd made jokes like that himself. In the not-so-distant past, even.

No more.

He got up. "Do you want to do the rest of the scene?" he offered. "It was going great."

Emily shook her head, her eyes shining. "Nope," she replied. "I think it's there, now."

"Cool."

"But there's something else I'd like to do." She got up. And for an instant, Pacey was sure she was going to come over to him and kiss him.

And the truly mind-boggling thing was, he almost wanted her to.

But she didn't.

Instead, she went to her closet and pulled out a big box of . . . something.

Pacey peered over her shoulder. "What's that?"

"For you," she told him. "I've never made this offer before, Pacey Witter. Not to anyone, ever. I want you to add something to 'Rant.' "

"It's not my piece!" Pacey protested, hands in the air. "Besides, art is one of my many short suits."

Her eyes held his, and she held out the box. "I want you to."

Pacey took the box, and Emily removed the top. Inside it were hundreds of photographs, clippings from newspapers, letters, cartoons, advertisements, flyers, and other things that Emily had selected out from an impossibly large assortment of published items.

"This is right up there in the amazing category," Pacey said.

"I'll take that as a compliment. Use anything you want and put it on 'Rant.' " She got busy removing the clips that held the acrylic guard over her artwork.

Pacey sat down with the box, shifting through the paper, looking for . . . what?

He didn't know.

"You'll know it when you see it," Emily said, still working with the acrylic. "Remember, I told you my middle name was Mindreader."

And there it was.

It was a clipping from an old newspaper, back in 1984. "No-Hitter and Drugs" was the headline. Pacey read in fascination a brief story about a pitcher for the Pittsburgh Pirates now working as an antidrug coordinator, who said that when he'd pitched in a no-hitter fourteen years before, he'd been hallucinating on LSD because he didn't think he'd been scheduled to pitch that day.

"I was so messed up that I tried to ruin everything I had just to prove I was as messed-up as I thought I was. And I almost succeeded, too. I almost threw it all away every time I threw that baseball, stoned out of my mind."

"I think I've found it," he told Emily.

"Put it up, then," she said. "Rubber cement's on my desk. Go easy with it."

Pacey stood in front of the mural. "Where should I put it?"

"Well, see, that's the scary part. You have to choose. And then you have to live with it."

Pacey stuck the clipping right above an article

about a woman who saw Elvis on her screen door and a photo of Halley's comet.

"I like it," Emily decided.

Pacey smiled. "Me, too. I also like you, Emily LaPaz."

"Pacey?"

"What?"

"It's wise to remember that ending a scene too cute is really the kiss of death. That's what my writing professor said, anyway."

Pacey nodded. "I'll try to keep that in mind."

"Maybe they *should* wreck the lighthouse and build that upscale mall and posh resort," Dawson muttered darkly to Jen, as his sneakers squished into yet another muddy part of the swamp that surrounded Dunn's Lighthouse. "Or better yet, a parking lot."

"Come on, Dawson," Jen said to him. "Where's your sense of adventure?"

"Back home with my boots."

"Hang in, the lighthouse is right there." She cocked her chin toward it. "I know you're dying of curiosity to see who my mystery guy is."

"We'll see if—hey!" Dawson ducked, as a bottle rocket whooshed overhead.

"We enter a war zone?" Jen asked.

"Quinn shot that at us!" Dawson realized, looking up at the top of the lighthouse.

"That's right, Dawson Leery!" Quinn called through a bullhorn. "What are you doing here?"

"I came with Jen," he yelled back, moving forward with trepidation in case any other small fireworks might zoom toward his head. "Are you out of your mind?"

"She was supposed to come alone. Besides, no men allowed!" Quinn bellowed. "Hi, Jen," she added in a much more friendly voice.

"Jen, I think this girl has had pigeons pecking at her cerebellum for too many days up there. We should leave."

"No men, Dawson!" Quinn bellowed again.

"What about Jen's date?" Dawson bellowed back.

*Unless* she's *Jen's mystery date,* Dawson thought. *Whoa.*

He pointed his video camera up at Quinn. "Quinn, what is your feeling about—"

Another bottle rocket sailed over his head.

"Quinn, can you please chill with the fireworks?" Jen demanded. "You could hurt someone!"

"When the enemy charges your moat, you fire on 'em," Quinn said.

Dawson's eyes slid over to Jen. "This girl is not normal, Jen."

Jen shrugged. "Neither am I."

"Look, I have nothing against homosexuals," Dawson said. "In fact, I'm reasonably certain that there's a strong biological imperative when it comes to—"

Jen laughed. "Wait, is this Dawson-speak for the fact that you think Quinn is my mystery date?"

"Don't you?"

"Hey, Quinn!" Jen called up to her. "Who is the one person you'd like to be stuck on a desert island with?"

"Ralph Nader," Quinn yelled down. "In Scott Speedman's body."

Jen looked at Dawson. "Major hetero."

"Dawson, you are banished!" Quinn called through her bullhorn. "I have more bottle rockets—"

"Don't shoot!" Dawson said. "I'm putting my camera equipment down now. Slowly. See?" Dawson laid his equipment at the base of the lighthouse.

"Good, because I don't want you filming, Dawson," Quinn warned him, "and I don't want you here."

"I was a little concerned for my friend Jen," Dawson said, his irritation rising. "Someone's been jerking her around all day. I was concerned that that someone could be someone who did not necessarily have her physical well-being in mind. Someone disturbed. Like an ax murderer. But I'm starting to think that that someone is you."

"Right, Dawson," Quinn said sweetly. "It's me, and I'm an ax murderer."

"She's kidding," Jen assured Dawson.

"Yes, I am," Quinn agreed pleasantly. "Want to know how you can tell?" She picked up her megaphone again. "IF I WAS AN AX MURDERER YOU'D BE AXED ALREADY, YOU IDIOT!"

Jen laughed, then bit her lip. "She has a point, Dawson."

He looked up. "Did you send her those notes?"

"Negative."

"Who did, then?"

"Ever see the cartoon where Bugs Bunny drops a thousand-pound weight out of a tower onto Elmer Fudd's head?" Quinn asked.

"Okay, all right, I'm leaving," Dawson said. He gave Jen a serious look. "But I'm waiting right back there in the swamp. If there's a problem, I want you to scream. You promise?"

"Dawson, there's not going to be a—"

"The horror movie options of the final reel of this little adventure are too numerous to enumerate," Dawson said. "So promise, or else—"

"I promise, I promise," Jen said. "There's a problem, I scream like I'm in *Scream 3*. Satisfied?"

"Barely." He looked up. "Quinn? I'm getting my camera and leaving now. Goodbye!"

"Bye, Dawson," Quinn told him. "When you're out of sight, Jen can come into my lighthouse."

*It's not your lighthouse*, Dawson was aching to tell her. *And if somehow we get lucky and raise enough money to buy this place, you should never be allowed up in it ever again, you psychotic, man-hating witch.*

"I'll be listening for you, Jen." Dawson got his camera equipment and started backing into the swamp.

"You may enter, now, Jen Lindley!" Quinn's amplified voice reached Dawson as he squished away through the mud. "Dawson is banished. Your real dream-date awaits."

*Chapter 12*

Joey's eyes slid over to Brett as the two of them walked down Main Street in the late afternoon sunshine. At their picnic, she'd mentioned to Brett that she needed to go to the drugstore to pick up a prescription for her nephew Alexander's ear infection, and Brett had volunteered to drive her there.

Amazing. He was going out of his way for her. And she'd just spent two hours with him at a picnic.

And she'd actually had a good time.

"Brett?"

"Huh?"

"I just wanted to say, I had a really nice time this afternoon."

He gave her a boyish grin. "No kiddin'?"

"No kidding."

His smile broadened. "Me, too, you know?"

She nodded. "I'm really glad I got a chance to know you. And it's helped me to realize something."

"What's that?"

"That you are not at all who I thought you were," Joey said. "And that I was just as guilty of judging you as the people I disdain for judging me."

Brett swaggered a little. "Cool."

"Cool," she agreed. They were in front of the drugstore. "Well, thanks for the picnic. And for the ride here. I guess I'll see you at the big celebrity auction party tonight, huh?"

"Count on it. Hey, how about I wait on you and give you a ride home?"

"You don't have to do that, Brett."

"Hey, pretend it's the one last thing you ordered me to do. I wanna make sure you got your entire fifty-one cents' worth."

"Okay, then. Thanks. I'll be right out."

Joey disappeared into the drugstore. Brett folded his arms and leaned against the building. He glanced down at his own shoes. They were a mess.

It figured. What a dummy. He'd shined everyone's shoes but his own.


"We're almost there," Emily told Pacey. They were in her car, heading toward Main Street. "Are you sure you don't want me to drive you to the emergency room?"

"I've had this before, it's just gas," Pacey managed, between groans. "The only thing I could die from is loss of dignity. I think it was that third container of bean dip with the corn chips."

"I made that dip myself," Emily sighed. "I'm really sorry."

"It was delicious," Pacey said. "But, ooh, I'm in some serious pain here."

The dip had been delicious. And the stomach pains had come over him shortly after he'd glued the article onto the "Rant" mural. He'd tried to ignore them, but within ten minutes the ache had gotten so bad that he'd gone running into Emily's bathroom to search for Pepto in the medicine chest.

He didn't find any. He looked everywhere he could think of. Nothing. No Pepto, no Gas-X, no Tums, no nothing that could help.

Zip.

Evidently the LaPaz family had strong stomachs.

Pacey groaned again. *Clearly this is cosmic revenge for having hidden out in her bathroom earlier to avoid the kissing scene.*

Confessing his gastrointestinal distress to Emily had been completely humiliating. But she'd been so gracious and easygoing about it, immediately offering to drive him to the drugstore for Gas-X salvation, that his admiration for her had risen even further.

Of course, at the moment the only thing rising was the acid lining his stomach.

Emily pulled into a parking space down the block from the drugstore. "I'll run in for you. What're you drinkin', Cowboy?" she teased.

"Double shot of Pepto and back it up with Gas-X," Pacey managed. "But I can get it myself."

"Pacey?"

"Yeah?"

"Relax."

Pacey's reponse was to open the car door with one hand and hold his stomach with the other.

Emily got out of the car and hurried around to him, hovering. "Are you sure you don't want to wait in my car, Pacey? I don't mind getting it for you."

"Thanks but I'm sure. I plan to medicate myself in aisle three like the desperate junkie I am. Be back soon." He lurched down the street, half bent over like his great-uncle in Maine with the really bad breath and even worse osteoporosis.

*No way James Dean ever went through this,* Pacey thought. *Can someone please explain why it is that the terminally cool do not get gas?*

Jen trudged up the dark, winding stone stairs of the lighthouse. Many of the stairs were chipped, some were nearly broken away completely. The treacherous climb was adding to her growing trepidation.

Because she had to admit it to herself, even though she'd never admit it to Dawson—this was really a little weird.

Scary, even.

She had no idea who was up in the lighthouse besides Quinn. Or why the person atop the stairs had been so secretive. Or what he wanted with her.

And then it occurred to her that if she was inside the lighthouse, and she really did scream for Dawson, he probably wouldn't be able to hear her.

*This is awful,* she thought. *I am such an—*

"You're almost to the top!" Quinn called. "Duck your head!"

"Don't tell me," Jen called back, "a bell is going to ring and then I get greeted by Quasimodo."

Panting a little, she ducked her head as Quinn had instructed in order to avoid clunking into some support beams and reached the top of the stairs.

In front of her was a wooden door.

Shut.

Jen's heart was pounding, and it wasn't from the climb.

*Here goes.*

Jen pushed the door open.

"For your information, *The Hunchback of Notre Dame* was set in the belltower of a big church and not in a lighthouse," Jen's mystery date said. "The Disney version was an insult to my intelligence. But the Charles Laughton version is a masterpiece."

"*Dina?*" Jen gasped, incredulously.

She stared at twelve-year-old Dina Wolfe, Chris's little sister. The geeky kid. The one with the massive crush on Dawson.

"It's me," Dina confirmed, as Quinn looked admiringly at the young girl.

"Those notes came from *you?*" Jen asked her. "You bid on me?"

Dina nodded. "Un-huh."

"You did it for your brother?" It was the only reason Jen could think of, not that it made any sense, either.

"Definitely not," Dina said firmly, folding her arms. "Not at all."

"Her brother actually came out here late one night," Quinn said, climbing into the room from her platform. "Supposedly to look for Dina. And then the sleaze tried to get me to let him in in order to put the moves on me."

Dina shrugged. "It's instinct with him. He's in terminal heat. Don't take it personally."

Jen sat heavily in an old cane-backed chair, one of the few pieces of furniture in the dank, empty space. Along one wall, near the window that looked out to sea, was Quinn's bedding, the pulley contraption that allowed her to bring up food, some books and magazines, a couple of flashlights, and a kerosene Coleman lantern.

Also a cell phone, Jen realized. And a box of bottle rockets.

"Okay," Jen began, turning her attention back to Dina and Quinn. "I'm completely and totally confused. This confusion could easily morph into unbelievable fury at any moment. So I would really like an explanation for all of this. Now."

"It's a little complicated," Dina hedged, her bravado slipping. She looked at Quinn for help.

"It's like this," Quinn said briskly. "Jen, Dina came out here a couple of weeks ago and I was like blah-blah-blah, some rich kid wants to gawk at Bigfoot—cut me a major break. Plus I was meditating, and she totally screwed up the energy flow to my chakras, which is exactly what I yelled down to her."

"Kindly cut to the chase," Jen suggested darkly.

"So, there was no one else around, and Quinn was bored I guess, and we started talking about meditation and the Dalai Lama and a lot of other cool stuff," Dina filled in. "It turned out we really had a lot in common. Like we both support the freedom movement in Tibet. We both like potato chips on peanut butter sandwiches. And—"

"In other words, we bonded like sisters," Quinn added. "I don't have a real little sister, either."

Jen threw her hands in the air. "Which has everything to do with me. Oh, now I understand!"

"I'm getting to that part," Dina said slowly.

"Get to it quickly, Dina," Jen snapped.

"All right. There's this guy I'm in love with. We were meant to be together for eternity. We're engaged."

Jen snorted. "You're twelve, Dina."

"I believe in long engagements," Dina explained seriously.

"And would this guy you're in love with be named Dawson Leery?" Jen asked.

"Affirmative. And before you say it, I know he doesn't know we're engaged. He doesn't know about the eternity part yet, either. You might even say that he doesn't appreciate me for the mature woman that I am."

Jen jumped up and strode to the wooden door. "You are a little girl, Dina. I don't know what's going on with you—or why you're helping her," she added sharply to Quinn. "But you can just leave me out of it. I'm outta here."

She started to open the door, hoping that Dawson was waiting not too far away.

"Please wait, Jen," Dina called. "Please? Can I just explain?"

Jen turned around, scowling. "You have thirty seconds, Dina. I mean it."

Dina inhaled deeply. Then all in one breath, she said:

"I know I look like a geeky little kid and guys my own age don't even pay any attention to me unless they want to copy my homework or something, but inside I'm not the person everyone sees on the outside and I really, really wanted, just once, to look really pretty. For Dawson."

Jen's tough-girl heart melted around the edges. "Oh Dina—"

"So I confided in Quinn," Dina went on, "about how I feel. And I asked her if she could do a makeover on me. You know. Like in the movies. Or on TV."

"Jen, I told Dina the truth. I haven't worn any cosmetics in three years," Quinn said, "to protest all the chemical additives and animal testing. Plus I'm not really good at any of those beauty things."

"But all those photographers who want to come out and take your pic—"

Quinn held up her hand. "They like that natural thing, I guess. But really, the last time I shaved my legs, it was to help stuff a pillow in protest of people wearing fur."

Jen made a face. "You stuffed a pillow with—"

"Let me tell you, it took the leg hair of, like, two thousand women. It was a publicity thing. Anyway," Quinn went on blithely, "I wanted to help Dina, but I wasn't the right person for the job. And then I thought of you."

Jen's jaw fell open. "Wait." She turned to Dina. "You bid on me so I could do a makeover on you? For Dawson?"

Dina hung her head, looking not twelve, but six.

"It was my idea that she ask you," Quinn said. "When you came out here to interview me, I noticed you had this really hip, confident look—the hair, the clothes, the makeup. I might not be into all of that myself, but, you know, high-maintenance femme bashing isn't my style."

"And I told her I knew you," Dina filled in. "That you went out with my brother once upon a time."

*Stayed in and got up close and personal with him in his hot tub, is more like it,* Jen thought. *Not one of the wisest choices I ever made.*

"You told me you were the one who made your grandma look so much younger and prettier that day at the winter fair," Dina went on earnestly, "so I thought maybe you could make me look prettier, too."

Jen sighed. "Look, Dina, I know it feels like you're going to be twelve forever, but you're not. I know all about wanting to grow up too fast and—"

"Excuse me, but you played this tape for me before and frankly it was really boring the first time," Dina said.

"But—"

"Anyway, I bid on you, and I won. Which means you're supposed to do what I tell you to do." Dina folded her arms expectantly, as if that were the end of the discussion.

"Even if you were fifteen or sixteen I'd still tell you that making yourself over for a guy never works," Jen said. "It's not the looks that matter."

"Uh, Jen?" Quinn asked.

"What?"

"She didn't bid on you for a lecture. She bid on you for a makeover. The secrecy and the notes and the cute guys bringing them to you, that was just something fun we dreamt up together."

"She gets really bored up here," Dina explained. "Did it work?"

"I mean, so what if Dina's twelve? She knows more than most adults I've had the misfortune to know," Quinn went on, not letting Jen answer Dina's question. "And so what if she wants to look pretty for Dawson Leery. Didn't you ever want to look beautiful for a boy you like?"

"Love," Dina corrected.

"Love," Quinn echoed. "Princess Dina is up here in my tower making wishes that I can't help her make come true. But you can. And I don't see what's so terrible about that, Jen. Really, I don't."

Jen took in Dina's hopeful, solemn face. She remembered being that young and insecure so well that the pain of it still felt like a fresh wound. Only no one had seen how much she was hurting. And it wasn't long after that that she began looking for affection in all the wrong places.

And from all the wrong people.

Jen cocked her head at Dina, studying her. "You've got lots of potential, you know."

Dina's face lit up. "I do?"

"Absolutely," Jen said. "Great eyes. Good bones."

"Then you'll do it?" Dina asked. "I've got makeup and hair stuff and a whole bunch of clothes back by the door over there and—"

"I'll do it on one condition," Jen interrupted. "I am not going to try and make you look sixteen."

"Why not?" Dina asked.

"Because you're twelve. But I will transform you into the cutest, hippest twelve-year-old in Capeside. Deal?"

Dina nodded. "Deal."

"Way cool deal," Quinn added happily.

Jen went to the window where Quinn usually sat and crawled out onto the platform. She picked up Quinn's bullhorn, which had been left out there.

"Yo, Dawson!" she called through Quinn's bullhorn.

"Don't tell him!" Dina hissed, panicked.

Jen waited as Dawson came crashing through the swamp, running to the base of the lighthouse.

"Are you okay?" Dawson yelled, as soon as he came into Jen's view.

"I'm fine. I just wanted to tell you you can go," Jen called.

"You sure?"

"Positive."

"Don't I get to film you and your mystery date?"

"Tonight at the big party," Jen promised. "See you."

Jen ducked back into the lighthouse and went over to Dina.

"All right, then," she told her. "It's time for the Anti–*Pretty Woman*, Anti–*She's All That*, Dina Wolfe Real Life Makeover."

They shook on it.

# Chapter 13

Joey stood in front of the pharmacy section of the drugstore, patiently waiting for Alexander's prescription, when she saw Pacey stagger into the store.

"Pacey! What's wrong?"

"The spirits of everyone I ever wronged are madly inflating helium balloons in my intestines," he managed, gingerly making his way down the aisle toward the medications for stomach upset.

"You look really terrible," Joey said.

"And I feel worse." He spotted the Pepto. "Ah, the love of my life. Speak to me!" He grabbed a bottle, tore off the protective plastic cover with his teeth, and wrenched open the bottle, popping a couple of Gas-X pills into his mouth at the same time.

Then, he guzzled like a man dying of thirst.

"Miss Potter, your prescription is ready," the pharmacist's assistant called.

"Oh, thanks. I'll be there in just a sec."

She watched Pacey as he wiped away his pink moustache with the back of his hand. "Better?"

Pacey closed his eyes. "Bliss is commencing even as we speak." He opened his eyes and sighed happily. "Whoever invented this stuff is a god."

"Right up there with Jonas Salk in the forefront of medical science," Joey said. She went to the counter and paid for Alexander's medication. It was so expensive. She and Bessie had no medical insurance now.

What if the kid got really sick?

Joey felt sick herself, just thinking about that possibility.

Pacey belched, less than discreetly, and Joey laughed.

"Nice to see that some of the old Pacey still lurks within."

"It's a well-kept secret that bodily functions exist even amongst perfect specimens of sensitive manhood such as myself." He rubbed his stomach. "What an improvement."

"Where's Emily LaPaz? Didn't she bid on you?"

"Waiting for me in her car," Pacey said. "Down the block."

"So, how was your day with her?"

Pacey considered before answering. "Illuminating," he finally said.

"That's a rather cryptic comment, Pacey. What did you guys do?"

"Hey, I'm supposed to be James Dean, remember? I owe it to my public to retain a certain air of mystery, which is exactly what I'm doing. So, moving on to you. How many ways did you find to humiliate the overgrown paramecium known as Brett Ardor?"

"Believe it or not, Pacey—and frankly I find this hard to believe myself—Brett Ardor actually has some redeeming qualities."

"In what parallel universe?" Pacey asked blithely.

"Just take my word for it. We actually talked. *Really* talked. It was . . . illuminating."

"Well, now that we're both well lit, we should return to our respective significant others," Pacey said, checking his watch. "For the next seven minutes, anyway. When Celebrity Auction Day officially ends."

Joey looped some hair behind her ear. "So, did Dawson video you and Emily?"

"She asked ever so casually," Pacey narrated, in his best voiceover tone. "And the answer is, not since Emily bid on me this morning. Why?"

Joey shrugged. "Just curious."

Pacey looked at her for a long time before he finally spoke softly.

"How long are you going to avoid him, Joey?"

"I don't want to talk about it."

"Funny, I could swear you were the one who just brought up his name."

"It's too . . . I can't . . ." Joey turned her head away. "Just drop it. Please."

*Everyone suffers. Joey. Dawson.*

"You got it," Pacey said, his voice softer. He draped an arm around Joey's shoulders. "Lemme pay for this bottled nectar of the gods and my salvation in pill form, and we're outta here."

He looked over at the checkout, where a long line of impatient people were waiting while a cashier-in-training painstakingly tried to ring up their purchases.

This could take forever.

*Everyone suffers, is right.*

Emily looked at her watch. Pacey had been gone a long time, and she was really starting to worry. What if it wasn't gas, and he had appendicitis or something?

She got out of her car and hurried toward the drugstore, but slowed down when she noticed who was standing outside.

Brett Ardor and a bunch of his friends.

The kings of cruel.

Well, she wasn't going to let that stop her. She'd just play deaf, dumb, and blind like she always did. Maybe she could even sneak into the drugstore without them seeing her and—

Chuck Owens, the infamous Upchuck, was leaning against his pickup truck picking lint out of his navel. He caught sight of Emily.

"Yo, look who's waddling into the store!" Upchuck yelled. "LaPig LaPaz!"

All the guys laughed. Emily cringed, but her face betrayed nothing. She reached for the door.

"Buyin' out the candy aisle, LaPig? Or the diet aids?" Brett asked.

Just at that moment, Joey and Pacey came out of the drugstore. It was clear from the furious looks on their faces that they had heard what Brett had just said.

Emily was rooted to the spot, too humiliated to move or speak.

Brett took in Joey's livid face. "Would you lighten up, Joey? So, she's got a moose caboose. Come on, it's funny!"

Joey's voice shook with fury. "No. It isn't." She longed to put her fist through his face. It took every ounce of her self-control not to do it.

"Hey, Ardor," Pacey called jovially, "speaking of funny, wanna hear something really funny? You're so dumb when you saw a sign that said 'Wet Floor,' you took a leak on it."

Brett's friends cracked up. Brett looked embarrassed, but managed to smile through it.

"In fact, Brett, you're so mentally deficient," Pacey went on, "that when you went to catch a plane and saw a sign that said 'Airport Left,' you went home."

Now Brett's friends were falling all over each other, they were laughing so hard. Two of them slapped each other five and hooted. "Come on, Brett, you gotta admit, it's funny!"

Brett wasn't laughing.

"Where's your sense of humor, Ardor?" Pacey asked. "C'mon, man, lighten up! You're so stupid, Brett, that—"

"Stop it, Pacey," Emily commanded sharply. "Just shut up."

Everyone turned to look at her in amazement.

No one had ever heard Emily LaPaz raise her voice before.

Emily's eyes held Pacey's. "You think that if you come up with insults that are more clever than his insults, that makes you better than him? Because guess what, Pacey? It doesn't."

"I was just trying to—"

"I know what you were 'just trying to,' " Emily said. "I don't need you to defend me just to feed your savior complex."

She turned and walked resolutely back to her car.

All Pacey could do was watch her walk away.

"His *what* complex?" Upchuck asked.

"Whatever," Brett said dismissively. He turned to Joey. "So, you ready to go?"

His friends razzed him and whistled. Upchuck wiggled his hips suggestively.

"Okay, the secret is out," Joey admitted. "Brett is the studliest of the studly. He and I have a really hot thing going on."

"We do?" Brett asked, his eyes lighting up.

"You don't have to hide it for my sake anymore, Brett," Joey said. "I fell in love with more than your massive, rippling muscles, you know."

"You did?"

She stared at him hard. "I fell in love with your sensitivity. Your kindness. The way you would never, ever, deliberately hurt someone."

She watched comprehension cross Brett's face. He even managed to look slightly guilty. And his buds were oddly quiet.

"It's kind of amusing, Brett, isn't it?" Joey went on.

"What is?"

"I actually had the illusion this afternoon that you were more than the Neanderthal peckerhead I had

always believed you to be. In fact, I berated myself
for judging you. Well, Brett, I would just like to
publicly state that I was wrong about you."

Brett looked utterly confused. "Huh?"

"You are not a peckerhead, Brett," Joey said.
"You are a total pecker, badly in need of emotional
Viagra. Because when it comes to simple human
kindness, Brett, you can't get it up. And I fault no
one but myself for ever thinking otherwise."

"Ha, dissed you!" Upchuck hooted.

"Shut up," Brett hissed to him. "Let's get out of
here."

Joey tapped Pacey on the shoulder.

"Huh?" He was watching Emily's car take off
down the street.

"I have to get this 'script home to Alexander,"
Joey told him. "I'll see you tonight at the party."

"Yeah."

"Listen, Pacey, about what Emily said. Don't be
too hard on yourself."

"She was right, though." Pacey finally turned to
Joey. "Emily was completely right about me."

"No one is ever completely right about anyone,
Pacey," Joey said. "Trust me on that one."

She left Pacey at the drugstore and made the long
trek home to the creek, rowed across it, and went
into her shabby, sad little house.

The living room was a mess. Bessie was sitting on
the couch, rocking Alexander.

"I got the—"

"Shhh." Bessie put a finger to her lips. "He's finally sleeping."

Joey put the bottle of antibiotics on the scarred

coffee table, and went back outside. She sat on her stoop and stared up at the endless, unfathomable evening sky.

It was starting to get dark. The first star was out. She thought about making a wish. Except that she no longer believed that wishes could come true.

Across the creek, Dawson sat on his front porch, staring up at the same sky. Missing the life he used to have. His parents together. With him in Capeside.

His Joey.

Her, most of all.

# Chapter 14

Usher's voice blasted from the sound system in the
school gym, which was already half-full of kids
who'd participated in the celebrity auction that day,
plus a lot of others who were just up for a party.

Dawson stood near the open doors, videoing people as they arrived. He'd been at it for over an hour,
making sure to arrive extra early so that he'd catch
the most people in the video.

And so he'd arrive before Joey.

*She can't very well walk by me and pretend I
don't exist,* he reasoned. *She'll have to say something. Then I'll say something. And then that
something could lead to . . . something else.*

An exceedingly lame plan, he realized. But for the
moment, it was the best he had.

Some of the "celebrities" had changed back into
regular clothes, others hadn't. Gaelynn showed up

142

with a bunch of other girls from the basketball team, and they had all dressed as Xena—Dawson got great footage of that. Greg Scott, the guy who had come in drag as Pamela Anderson, was still in drag, and he had new water-balloon breasts, even larger than the first pair he had.

*I guess some things are very hard to give up,* Dawson thought dryly.

And then he thought, *Joey would find that hilarious.*

Chris Wolfe, no longer in his Elvis rags, rounded the corner, smiling hugely when he saw that Dawson was filming him. Amazingly, on his arm was—of all people—Bitsy Bannerman, in a pink-and-white slip dress, carrying a little pink cellphone with a tiny pink purse dangling from it.

"So, Chris, you were the great one himself today," Dawson said from behind the camera. "Did you enjoy impersonating an icon?"

"Let's face it, the guy was kind of bloated and kind of overrated," Chris replied. "But hey, it was a charity thing." He flashed a movie-star smile directly into Dawson's camera.

"You didn't participate in the event today, did you?" Dawson asked Bitsy, even though he was well aware of the answer.

"I was kind of too busy," Bitsy said. "Plus, no offense, but I think it was a big waste of time. Plus, no offense, but I don't take questions from Screenplay Videos."

"Why is that?" Dawson asked.

"Don't joke with me, Dawson. For one thing, if I'd known that my mother had hired you and Pacey for her party, I would have made sure that you'd been fired. And for another thing, how much money did you actually raise with your lame-o auction?"

"Pacey's going to announce that later," Dawson said impassively.

Bitsy ran a hand over her perfectly straight, smooth hair. "Look, it's not going to matter, because—"

"Bitsy! Oh my God, you look so *cute!*" one of her sycophantic friends squealed, running over to hug her as Dawson filmed the two of them. Bitsy kissed her friend on one cheek, then the other, as if she were French.

"This is such a hoot, isn't it?" Bitsy asked her friend. "Us, at a party in the Capeside High gym?"

"Totally," her friend agreed. "It's so, like, *Happy Days* or something!"

"Shall we go in, ladies?" Chris asked them, holding out his arms.

They each took one of his outstretched arms, Chris winked into Dawson's camera, and the threesome went into the gym.

"You think Wolfe is gonna do both of 'em?" a voice from behind Dawson asked. "If you got the bucks, man, you're a babe magnet, no matter what."

Dawson turned around.

Brett Ardor. Who had spent the entire day with Joey.

That Joey had been in the solo company of so loathsome a human specimen as Brett Ardor when she wasn't even speaking to him, Dawson, was beyond infuriating.

144

Dawson turned his camera on Brett. "Have fun today, Ardor?"

" 'Z-okay."

"You were certainly proficient at those shoeshines this afternoon, Brett. Could that be your future career path?"

"Ha-ha," Brett barked. "Real funny."

"No humor intended," Dawson assured him from behind his camera. "Surely when a man is as gifted with spit and polish as you are, and with such obvious limitations as to clearly eliminate any future that might call for a three-digit IQ—"

"Hey, lemme tell you something." Brett put his face right up to the lens of Dawson's camera.

"Tell away. I hang on your every word."

"Okay," Brett said. "This is a whatchamacallit. A riddle."

"Yes?"

"What do you call a real clever dis with big words?"

"I don't know, Brett," Dawson said. "What do you call a real clever dis with big words?"

Brett stabbed his finger at the camera. "A *dis*, man," he said. "A dis." Brett smiled, then turned and lost himself in the crowd.

Dawson watched him leave. "I have a feeling that was supposed to be profound," he murmured to himself.

"Hey, Dawson."

It was Jen, with Jack. She looked really great and very Jenish in something sheer and short.

"I see you've returned safely from both *Plesant-ville* and the lighthouse," Dawson noted.

She nodded. "Thanks for going out there with me. I mean it."

He raised his camera. "So, I'm dying of curiosity. Who did your mystery date turn out to be?"

"Not telling," Jen said.

He put the camera down. "You're kidding."

"Nope."

Dawson looked at Jack. "Do you know who it was?"

"Yep." Jack cheerfully clapped Dawson on the shoulder. "Catch you later."

He and Jen headed into the party. "Save me a dance, Dawson," Jen called back to him over her shoulder.

"Great. Fine. Wonderful. You got it," Dawson declared, seething.

"Yo, Dawson, you're talking to yourself," Pacey said, coming over to him.

"Thank you for pointing that out to me, Pacey. Tonight I seem to be the best company I can come up with."

"Uh-huh." Clearly Pacey had barely heard him. He craned his neck around the room. "Hey, have you seen Emily?"

"LaPaz?"

"You know another Emily?"

"No, Pacey. I don't. I barely know that Emily. And no. I haven't seen her. Why do you ask?"

"Hey, yeah, have fun, Dawson," Pacey said, hurrying off to find Emily.

"Well, this evening just keeps getting better and better," Dawson said. Glumly, he turned back to the door. Screenplay Videos on the job. Make sure you get footage on everyone. Heather Phillips with Mark Cabberus. Upchuck Owens with a bunch of his equally vomitous friends. Emily LaPaz with Joey Potter.

*Emily LaPaz with Joey?*

Joey.

Wearing a long, simple white cotton dress Dawson clearly remembered from the summer before. They'd gone to an outdoor concert. And then for a walk by the pier. All the stars had been out. He'd told her how beautiful she looked, that her eyes shone even brighter than the stars. And he didn't mind at all when she'd wrinkled her nose and pointed out just how trite his compliment was. And that a budding genius such as Dawson Leery really should work a little harder to come up with something original.

And she'd laughed when he'd stopped her critique with a kiss, and then . . .

God. And then.

"Good evening!" Dawson called to them, his voice a shade too bright. "Care to make a save-the-lighthouse statement for the video?"

"Not really," Emily said, smiling sweetly.

"How about you, then?" Dawson turned the camera on Joey.

"I think you know the answer to that, Dawson."

He put the camera down. "Minds change, Joey. It's been known to happen."

Her face was unreadable. He turned to Emily. "Pacey has been looking for you all over, by the way."

"He has?"

Dawson nodded. "He headed that way, seeking you out, just a few minutes ago."

Emily looked over at Joey. "Go ahead," Joey told her. "It's fine." Emily hurried off.

"So. I didn't know you and Emily were friends," Dawson said.

"We're not, really. I mean I don't know her. We kind of met up this afternoon. I like her." Joey was as to the point as possible.

"So." Dawson pressed on. "How was your date with Brett Ardor?"

"It wasn't a date, Dawson. As you very well know."

"He said something very strange to me before. It was supposed to be a riddle, he said. Something about how if you dis someone using big words, it's still a dis. Whatever that means."

Joey smiled slowly. "He said that?"

That old demon jealousy took Dawson by the throat. That Brett Ardor could bring that smile to her face!

"What, is it supposed to be deeply meaningful?" Dawson asked, an edge to his voice. "Did Brett Ardor prove that behind his dumb jock facade beats the heart of a sensitive and misunderstood poet?"

"I thought exactly that, Dawson," Joey said.

"I knew it."

"For about five deluded minutes. Everyone isn't sensitive and deep and vulnerable underneath their well-constructed facade, Dawson."

"No?"

"No," Joey went on. "The truth is, sometimes a

cigar is just a cigar. And sometimes a dumb jock is just a dumb jock."

She looked him dead in the eye. "And sometimes, even when two people are sensitive and deep and vulnerable underneath their well-constructed facade, they need that facade, Dawson. So that they don't shatter into a million tiny, little pieces. And then blow away."

His eyes held hers. "For how long?"

"As long as it takes," she replied. Then she walked away.

# Chapter 15

Pacey pushed through the throng of kids.

"Hey, can I have everyone's attention?" Pacey called, when he got to the live microphone on the small stage. The music ended, and slowly, people turned their attention to Pacey.

"We had a really successful event today, and for a really great cause. I want to thank everyone who got involved with this because it was the hard work of a whole lot of—"

"Can the speech, Witter!" someone yelled. "How much money did we make?"

Pacey looked slightly uncomfortable. "A lot. We can feel really proud. I mean it."

"How much?" someone else yelled impatiently.

"Twelve hundred dollars," Pacey admitted. "But we're expecting some more donations. And when Dawson gets his video edited, I'm sure it will bring in—"

"That ain't squat," Upchuck yelled.

Pacey turned to him. "Look, none of us went into this thinking we were going to raise three hundred thousand dollars on our little pretend-celeb day, okay? The point is, we did something. We didn't just leave it to someone else. So, yes, I'm sure that the Bannermans' Summer Lights fund-raiser brought in the big bucks that will, hopefully, save Dunn's Lighthouse. But we're all a part of it. And I think we should feel great about that."

"How much did the Bannermans' fund-raiser bring in?" Heather called out.

"In udder verds, Pacey," Uma added, in her Swedish accent, "are ve savink ze lighthouse or not?"

"Actually, I haven't heard from the Bannermans yet, so I don't know how much or who they're donating it to," Pacey admitted. A bead of sweat popped out on his forehead. "That is, they have yet to return my phone call. I'm sure they will. But they haven't. Yet."

"Uh, excuse me, excuse me, but I think I can speak for the Bannermans," Bitsy Bannerman cried, as she worked her way up to the stage.

"May I?" she asked Pacey, pointing to the microphone. "I think I can clear all this up."

Pacey stepped back and folded his arms as Bitsy stepped up the stairs that led to the stage.

"Okay, hi," Bitsy said into the microphone. "For those of you who don't know me, I'm Bitsy Bannerman. My parents are—"

"How much did they raise?" Upchuck bellowed.

"I'm here to make an announcement, actually,"

Bitsy said. "While the blind auction went really well and made lots of money, my parents have reconsidered their position on this issue."

A murmur went through the crowd.

"Okay, the shopping mall thingie that was going to be built was tacky," Bitsy went on. "And my parents put together more than enough funds at their party to form a group that will buy the property from the Dunns and stop construction of the mall. That land is going to be, like, a nature preserve or something."

People applauded.

Clearly, though, more info was forthcoming. Bitsy was happy to supply it.

"As for the part of the land where the lighthouse actually sits, my parents have decided to buy that part from the Dunns and build a new family estate. We might even leave the lighthouse standing in the center of our property, and, you know, get the architects to build the estate so it looks old and matches it and everything."

Dead silence in the gym.

"So, okay, I know it's not exactly what you guys wanted," Bitsy said. "But it's a lot better than Woodman Corporation getting it and putting in a mall, isn't it? We think you'll see that in the long run. And I just want to say on behalf of the Bannerman family that we're really proud to have all of you as our neighbors."

She turned to Pacey. "Oh, you can, like, donate the twelve hundred dollars you raised for any charity you guys want. Thanks for listening, you guys. Really."

Bitsy stepped perkily away from the microphone and headed off the stage.

But Jen reached her first, and blocked her path.

"Are you telling us that your family *stole* Dunn's Lighthouse?"

"My parents are going to call it Bannerman-Dunn's Lighthouse," Bitsy explained, "so I don't know what you're so bent out of shape about." She stepped neatly around Jen and went to join her friends.

Pacey felt sick to his stomach. And this time, no amount of Pepto was going to alleviate the feeling.

He walked heavily to the microphone. "All I can say is, I'm sorry," he told the stunned crowd. "I'll make sure that everyone gets a refund of every penny they spent. I really wanted this to be something great. And I guess . . . I guess I failed. And I'm really sorry that—"

"PACEY WITTER," came an amplified female voice. "I WANT TO OFFER MY CONGRATULATIONS."

The voice had come from the back of the gym.

Everyone spun around. There stood Quinn Bickfee, a bullhorn to her lips, looking impossibly, naturally gorgeous.

And standing next to her was twelve-year-old Dina Wolfe. Only, not even Chris could be sure it was his little sister. Because the geeky, awkward ugly duckling had been transformed into a sleek-haired, shining-faced swan. Dina waved one hand at the crowd, slowly and from the wrist, the way Queen Elizabeth always did.

"Great to see you, Quinn," Pacey said into the microphone, "but—"

"You forgot someone." Quinn pointed to Dina.

"And great to see you, Dina," Pacey added. "I wish I had some good news so that I could accept your congratulations, Quinn. But unless your name happens to be Bannerman, we're a little short on good news. They're buying Dunn's Lighthouse right out from under everyone. So why aren't you still up there?"

Quinn strode onto the stage and took the microphone from Pacey, Dina trotting after her.

"Hi," Quinn said into the mike. "I guess you all know who I am." She flashed her perfect smile. She was, after all, a celebrity. And they were, after all, the first people to see her down from the lighthouse. Dina crowded in close so that she'd end up in the photos, too.

"I have an announcement to make," Quinn said from the stage. "Thank God for cellular telephones. I want to announce that I have just sold my pitch for *Lighthouse Girl*, to Deidre Carr Productions who will be making it into a TV movie for Lifetime."

Stunned silence.

"I'll be playing myself in the movie," Quinn added modestly.

"Never thought of that angle," Jen murmured to Dawson.

"Well, the role of the lighthouse is still open," Dawson replied wryly.

"What does that do for the lighthouse?" someone called out.

Quinn smiled beatifically. "In a bidding war for

my pitch, arranged by my new agents at William Morris," Quinn went on, "I'll be receiving half a million dollars for the deal. Three hundred thousand of those dollars are to be paid directly to the Nature Conservancy, which has arranged to purchase all the property from the Dunns. And here's my faxed deal memo to prove it."

Quinn waved a piece of paper in the air, as absolute pandemonium broke out. People were jumping up and down, screaming with happiness, cheering and applauding. Bitsy turned and stomped out, muttering darkly to herself, as her friends followed her like little ducklings. Chris Wolfe stayed behind, though. Sometimes even scoring wasn't worth putting up with the Bitsy Bannermans of the world.

Someone blasted vintage Doors through the sound system, and the party went into joyous overdrive.

"I bet it was the Dina makeover part of the story that sold it," Jen said, smiling at Jack who stood nearby. "Damn, I'm good. Excuse me a sec."

Jen worked her way over to Dawson, to see how he was taking to the new Dina. His face was hidden behind his video camera as he filmed Quinn and Dina posing.

"Doesn't she look cute?" Jen asked him.

"Quinn's beautiful," Dawson said.

"I meant *Dina*."

"Yes, actually. She's not scowling for once."

Jen rolled her eyes. "Men are so obtuse."

"I think I want to be Quinn when I grow up," Jen told Dawson.

"She's amazing," he agreed. "I wonder what Joey thought about—"

"Dawson?"

He turned to Jen, his eyebrows raised in question.

"Kindly focus. See that little girl up there desperately pretending that she's just like Quinn?"

"Dina?" Dawson asked.

"Right on the first try. I spent exactly two hours and thirty-seven minutes transforming her this afternoon."

Awareness dawned. "You mean Dina—?"

Jen nodded. "She bid on me secretly because she wanted a makeover. She and Quinn got to be friends, and Quinn helped her plan it. I was chosen as fairy godmother."

"Amazing." Dawson chuckled. "I have to admit, Jen, I never, ever would have guessed that Dina Wolfe was your mystery date."

"She isn't my mystery date," Jen said. "She's yours."

"She—?"

"Did it for you, Dawson," Jen filled in. "She's convinced that you're her Prince Charming. And yes I know she's only twelve. And yes I know she can be irritating and impossible. But a fairy godmother can only do so much. Once Cinderella gets to the ball, the ball is in Prince Charming's court."

"I feel utterly unworthy of what she feels for me, Jen," Dawson said.

"You probably are utterly unworthy of it. None of us are worthy of that kind of love. That's what makes it so incredible."

Dawson carefully put his camera on a chair. Then

he walked over to Dina. She stared up at him, mute. "You look beautiful," he told her.

Her usual scowl flitted across her face. "You don't have to say that."

"I said it because it's true." He bowed to her. "Dina Wolfe, may I have this dance?"

All she could do was nod. He took her hand, and led her to the center of the floor. The music changed abruptly to a slow, romantic ballad.

"Slow dances are better," Dina told him.

"Well then, it's a great coincidence that one just started," Dawson said.

"Actually, I slipped that white guy with the dreads twenty bucks to put on a slow song if he saw you and me on the dance floor," Dina admitted.

Dawson laughed. "You're going to be dangerous one of these days, Dina Wolfe."

"I'm dangerous now, Dawson Leery."

She reached up and tried to wrap her arms around his neck. He gently put them into a more formal dance hold, with plenty of daylight between them.

And they danced.

"Emily!" Pacey exclaimed. She was outside, behind the gym, sitting on a large rock near a grove of trees, looking up at the stars. Pacey hurried over to her. "I've been looking for you everywhere."

"And now you've found me," Emily said. "Nice night, huh?"

"The best." Pacey sat down on the closest boulder. "I can't believe what Quinn did. It's mind boggling, really. I doubt that if someone handed me a half mill for the Pacey Witter Story. I'd use it to save a lighthouse."

"Oh, you never know," Emily said. "You may be more heroic than you give yourself credit for."

Pacey folded his arms. "You busted me this afternoon."

"I had no right to say what I said—"

"No, no, you were right," Pacey said. "Pacey Witter riding in on his white horse wasn't what you needed. It was what I needed."

She didn't say anything. In the distance, he could hear some kids laughing. Over by the trees, Heather Phillips was in heavy mack mode with Chris Wolfe.

*You just never know*, Pacey thought, watching them. *She spent the day finding ways to humiliate him. And now—*

*Attraction is a bizarre, uncontrollable, indefinable thing.*

Emily cleared her throat. "Actually, Pacey, I went looking for you earlier," she said. "But then I chickened out. Which leads me to my cheap and tawdry confession."

She wasn't looking at him, and her voice was so low he wasn't even positive he'd heard what he thought he'd heard.

"I overheard you tell someone that you were going to come to the auction as James Dean," Emily went on. "I didn't write that scene at writing camp. I wrote it the night before the auction. So I could do it with you."

"You did?"

"Did you really think that your avoidance of acting out that scene with me wasn't totally and painfully obvious? I was acutely aware that the thought of kissing me did not exactly fill you with anticipation."

"Then why did you put yourself through that?" Pacey asked quietly.

"Good question, Pacey. When I figure out the answer, I'll add the appropriate poetic metaphor for it to 'Rant.' "

Some people tumbled out of the gym. Heather and Chris headed for his car, their arms around each other.

"You know, I never did get a chance to really critique the writing in your scene," Pacey said.

"Forget it, Pacey."

"No, no, this could be really helpful to you. I've been helping refine Dawson's work for years."

Emily looked at him, and smiled. "Okay, script critic, let's hear it."

"Okay," Pacey echoed. "Peter admitted his vulnerability to Esme, right? And in the rewrite, she tells him that she's just as scared and vulnerable as he is. Which is this big revelation, because he thinks she's so strong—"

"What's your point, Pacey?"

"I'm getting to it," Pacey said, "and it's just possibly brilliant, so go with it. Okay, so we've got these two vulnerable people. But we don't get to see Peter's character change."

"Change how?" Emily asked.

"Like when he realizes that the connection he feels for Esme could, to his own surprise, be more than just platonic friendship. When he sees this mural she did, this mind-bogglingly incredible mural, and then he begins to see her, really *see* her, for the first time. And he realizes what a truly incredibly beautiful woman she is. A desirable woman. Whom he desires."

Slowly, she turned to him.

Pacey touched her hair. He smiled into her eyes. And then, he gently, tenderly, and very passionately, kissed Emily LaPaz.

Finally, they broke apart.

"I have a critique of your critique," Emily said.

"What's that?"

"Well, let's assume that Esme knows that Peter is in love with . . . oh, let's call her Annie. She respects that. And she knows the kiss they're sharing is just one single perfect moment that doesn't belong to their past or their future. But how does Esme know if Peter is only kissing her as part of his savior complex, not because he really desires her?"

"She'd know by looking into his eyes," Pacey said.

Emily's eyes searched his. She smiled. "You're right," she said.

Pacey took her hand, gave it a gentle squeeze, and then let go.

"I know."

Dawson sat arms folded in the darkened video room at school, watching the raw footage he'd taken that day. After spending an hour as Dina's Prince Charming, her mother had shown up to take her home. Thankfully.

And after that, he just hadn't felt like he belonged.

Anywhere, really. And the anyone he belonged with didn't want him anymore.

*So here I am, hanging out once again in the cozy, dark video womb I know and love,* Dawson thought.

Joey's face appeared on the monitor. She was laughing about something. Then glaring at him. God, you could read every emotion on her face. He knew the meaning of every tiny tic, every blink, every tilt of her head.

He reran the Joey footage. The he fast forwarded to her arrival at the party that night, with Emily.

There was Joey, in that white dress.

"I think you know the answer to that, Dawson," she was saying.

He rewound it so he could watch it again. And was so intent that he didn't hear the door quietly open just a crack.

Joey had wandered away from the dance, overcome by a terrible loneliness. She wanted. A lot of things she'd never have.

A different father.

No. Her father. Who made different choices.

And Dawson. She wanted—

That one was tougher. All she knew for sure was that she didn't want to hurt so much anymore.

She figured she'd find him here, in the video room. She wasn't surprised that her premonition was right. So she watched him, watching her on the monitor. Maybe the flickering video images of her were more real to him than she was.

He rewound the tape and watched her again.

An ache filled Joey's throat, a deep longing for

the time when she'd still believed that Dawson's love could make everything okay.

But that Joey was gone. And the new Joey, whoever she was becoming, was a half-developed photograph. Even she didn't know how she would turn out.

She tiptoed back to the door, about to exit, when the light from the hallway glinted on Dawson's open backpack on the table.

And there, sticking out of it, was a drawing of Quinn Bickfee in Dunn's Lighthouse by Joey Potter.

*He bought my sketch at the silent auction*, she realized. *And he never even told me.*

Carefully, Joey let herself out of the video room. She walked out of the school, into the crisp night air.

"Thank you so much for buying my drawing, Dawson," she told the starry sky. "And for not even trying to impress me by telling me that you bought it. Thank you so much."

She wrapped her arms around herself, gave herself a gentle squeeze, and smiled.

# About the Author

C. J. Anders is the pseudonym for a well-known young adult fiction-writing couple.

# ROSWELL HIGH

**He's not like other guys.**

**Liz** has seen him around. It's hard to miss Max—the tall, blond, blue-eyed senior stands out in her high-school crowd. So why is he such a loner?

**Max** is in love with Liz. He loves the way her eyes light up when she laughs. And the way her long, black hair moves when she turns her head. Most of all, he loves to imagine what it would be like to kiss her.

But Max knows he can't get too close. He can't let her discover the truth about who he is. Or really, what he is....Because the truth could kill her.

One astounding secret...a shared moment of danger...life will never be the same.

A new series by Melinda Metz

Available from Archway Paperbacks
Published by Pocket Books

2034